"No one here knows who I am."

Charles answered a question she had not yet asked. "My trainer calls me Charles Smith when introductions are unavoidable, which is why your own last name was less than believable."

"Just because Smith is a common name doesn't mean it's a false one," Valerie said, swallowing her guilt. "Not everyone assumes a fake identity."

"Not everyone. Only those who can't find privacy any other way, and those who wish to deceive."

"A deception in either case," she countered. "So why didn't you introduce yourself to me as Charles Smith?"

He smiled ruefully. "I've been asking myself the same question." He looked directly into her eyes, and she held her breath. "Let's just say I misjudged you and those dazzling eyes of yours."

MELINDA CROSS would love her readers to believe she was kidnapped as a child by an obscure nomadic tribe and was rescued by a dashing adventurer. Actually, though, she is a wonderfully imaginative American writer who lives in a restored Dutch Colonial farmhouse with her husband—a true romantic, although he won't admit it. Every spring, without fail, when the apple orchard blooms, he gathers a blanket, glasses and wine and leads Melinda out to enjoy the fragrant night air. Romantic fantasy? Nonsense, she says. This is the stuff of real life.

Books by Melinda Cross

These books may be available at your local bookseller.

Don't miss any of our special offers. Write to us at the following address for information on our newest releases.

Harlequin Reader Service
901 Fuhrmann Blvd., P.O. Box 1397, Buffalo, NY 14240
Canadian address: P.O. Box 2800, Postal Station A,
5170 Yonge St., Willowdale, Ont. M2N 6J3

MELINDA CROSS

a very private love

Harlequin Books

TORONTO • NEW YORK • LONDON
AMSTERDAM • PARIS • SYDNEY • HAMBURG
STOCKHOLM • ATHENS • TOKYO • MILAN

Harlequin Presents first edition June 1986
ISBN 0-373-10889-3

Original hardcover edition published in 1985
by Mills & Boon Limited

CHAPTER ONE

VALERIE wriggled deeper into her seat as the thrust of the 747's engines strained to lift the jumbo jet into the air. She squeezed her eyes shut until her forehead wrinkled, fighting the sickening awareness that she was leaving the ground in a machine weighing tens of thousands of pounds, and that it was perfectly preposterous that anything that heavy could fly.

She had flown more hours than any hundred other women her age, and still the fear was with her; the growing, frightening certainty that she was pushing the percentages; that every additional uneventful flight increased the odds against the next, and that soon it would be her turn.

The thick coil of her bun pushed a hairpin into the back of her neck as she pressed her head against the seat, but she welcomed the distraction of pain, and remained rigid, long tapering fingers clutching the armrests with a pressure that whitened her knuckles.

Her normally delicate, porcelain colouring was starkly white with tension, and in her immobility, she resembled a marble likeness of a woman, sculpted lovingly by an idealistic artist into lines of cold, lifeless elegance.

As the jet levelled and the engine noise receded, she opened brilliant, large eyes the same colour as the warm toast of her hair, and her face became immediately alive, and somehow childishly vulnerable. The plane lurched through a solitary air pocket, and she concentrated on smoothing her forehead, or thinking of something else. Her thoughts backtracked to the previous morning.

She had grumbled a complaint when her editor had

finished outlining her assignment. 'John, come on. Why can't Scott take it, or Terry? They love this sort of thing. Besides, they both own horses. They'd know what to look for. I'll be lost on an assignment like this.'

John had lowered bushy eyebrows in one of his famous facial reprimands. 'You didn't know anything about economic summit meetings either, and I didn't hear you complaining about that assignment.'

'That was different. That was news, hard news. This is . . . well, for Heaven's sake, John. It's a *horse* show. What's the *American Bulletin* doing covering a horse show, anyway? That's a local colour piece. You'll knock us right off the news-stands with that kind of county fair coverage.' She pouted prettily, but to no effect. If anything, John looked even more stern.

'Turn off the puppy dog eyes, Valerie. I'm immune. And just because your father and I were brothers doesn't give you licence to question my business judgment. None of my other journalists would dare do that. You may be a pretty fair reporter working for one of the country's top news magazines, but you're still the same brat who spit strained peas all over my dinner jacket when you were a year old. I knew how to handle you then, and I know how to handle you now. I'm the editor, you're the journalist, and don't forget it!'

Even ranting, as he was then and as he did often, John's affection for his niece was painfully obvious, and she had allowed him to continue uninterrupted, an indulgent smile playing about her lips.

'Besides, Valerie, this is not just a horse show; it's a news story. You've had your head in the sand again, ignoring the news that goes on all around you, seeing only the obvious. If you'd been doing your homework, you'd know that the wealth of this country is funnelling rapidly from Wall Street into barns from one coast to the other, and there hasn't been an investment as profitable as the Arabian horse since they found the first nugget in

Sutter's Creek. These horses are selling for upwards of a million dollars apiece, and if that isn't news, I don't know what is. Now go pick up your tickets from Marjorie and get the hell out of here.'

She had hesitated at the door on her way out of his office, only a little miffed at the lecture. 'Why me?' she had asked seriously, knowing as she always did that his reasons would be absolutely sound. 'Why not Scott or Terry? They're both excellent journalists, and they both love horses.'

John had put on the same face of resigned tolerance he had worn often when she was a child, in patient response to her endless, infantile questions. 'For just that reason. They know horses, they love the horse business, and theirs would be a view from the inside. You hate the monsters and you know nothing. You'll be objective, like most of our readers, and you won't be sidetracked by any sentimental fascination. You'll *make* it a news story, not just a horse show. And that's what I want.'

She had smiled at the reasoning, flawless, as she had expected. 'All right. Under that premise, I'll cover it. But I won't like it.' She had blown him a kiss on the way out. 'See you in a week, Uncle John!'

'Don't call me uncle!' he had roared as she closed the door, smiling.

She smiled again now, remembering the boom of his voice, a comforting sound that had been part of her life ever since her parents had been killed when she was three. A plaster-cracking roar, John's verbal expressions of anger had intimidated more servants than she could remember during her growing years in the elegant New York bachelor brownstone. Timid and mousey, or pompous, and stuffy, they had come and gone in an unending procession, either terrified or indignant when John's sudden and frequent bursts of outrage shook the chandeliers. But to Valerie, the sound meant security. John was home, raising the roof perhaps, but home none the less; ready to wrap her in a bear hug, help with her schoolwork, or listen endlessly in that silent, earnest way of his.

"The bar is open, Miss. Would you care for a cocktail? A soda?'

'What? Oh. Juice, please. Grapefruit, if you have it.'

The stewardess moved on down the narrow aisle, taking other orders, and Valerie lurched out of the reverie that had saved her from the disconcerting sensation of being airborne.

'You hate flying, don't you?' The voice came from the bank of seats to her right, followed shortly by the extension of a broad, male hand across the aisle. 'Jacob Lancer,' the voice identified himself, and she looked up at one of the most extraordinarily handsome faces she had ever seen.

She smiled willingly, eager to be distracted from the privacy of her own thoughts. They would wander for a time, she knew, then inevitably focus on her instinctive fear of flight, leaving her shivering and nauseous. 'I do,' she admitted. 'I hate to fly. Valerie Kipper.' She slid her small hand into his, and felt the firm, warm pressure of controlled strength.

'Not *the* Valerie Kipper, surely?'

'You know the name?'

'If you're the Kipper who covered the McArvie trial for the *American Bulletin*, I do. And the Mexico City Conference of Kings?'

She nodded, pleased that her pieces had been memorable enough to call attention to her byline.

'Then I most certainly know the name. What a pleasure this is! May I?' He indicated the vacant seat to her left, and she inclined her head in permission.

She tried to stifle the familiar question, tried to keep it locked safely away in the recesses of her mind, but still it came. Is this the one? Is this finally the one?

All her life she had believed without question that when she met the man she was destined to love, she would know it immediately. It was a childish notion, a leftover from fairytales, but she couldn't let it go. Perhaps it was because she had never really experienced a family situation that the idea of marriage and children was so tantalising. It certainly wasn't fashionable. Today's women longed for precisely the kind of life Valerie already had: a brilliant career, a promising future, and the freedom of a single woman. The few she had confided in scoffed at her secret wish for a lifelong love, and she learned quickly to keep her daydreams to herself, safe from the ridicule of others. But she who had intimidated men for most of her twenty-five years, either because of her beauty, her position, or a combination of the two, still believed that somewhere in the world was one man she would not intimidate, one man she could give herself to completely. It made her particularly attentive to each man she met, and with this one, as with others before him, she found herself asking, is this the one?

She liked his face. Totally open, almost preposterously American. He had the bronzed good looks of a man who worked outside: sandy hair with streaks almost white where the sun had lightened it, and the strong, clean profile of a perfectly conditioned athlete, whose face reflects the health of his body. He was more muscular than she expected when he stood and crossed in front of her to take the empty seat, and she was totally unprepared for the eyes whose colour had been nondescript with the glare of the window behind him. She voiced her amazement without thinking.

'Your eyes are the most incredible colour I've ever seen!'

His grin was almost rueful, and infectious. 'Ridiculous, aren't they? My claim to fame. The only thing people always remember about me. Oh yes, they say, I know him . . . Jacob What's-his-name, the man with the periwinkle eyes.'

'That's it! That's exactly the colour they are!'

'And that's what my mother had them put on my birth certificate. Not blue, not hazel, but periwinkle. Don't know how she managed it, or why they didn't change to a more acceptable colour, but . . .' He shrugged good-naturedly, and she began to like the man as much as she liked his face. 'So tell me,' he prompted, 'why are you afraid of flying? You must do it often, with your career.'

'I fly a lot,' she answered, but it doesn't get easier. My parents were killed in a plane crash.'

He turned his head quickly to face front, and she could see the regret in the sudden tightening of his jaw. 'I'm really sorry. I have this incredible knack for asking all the wrong questions.'

'No, no, please don't let it bother you. It was an innocent question, and it was a long time ago. I was only three at the time.'

His lips curved into an agreeable smile as he faced her once again. 'Okay. We'll start over. Do you mind talking? I've been on planes for the last week, alone mostly. A real conversation would be nirvana for me right about now. Are you on an assignment?'

'I am,' she nodded. 'Not one I chose, unfortunately. My editor is a tyrant. Sent one of his best journalists out to cover a horse show.'

'Really.'

'Really. Some Arabian horse affair in Lexington. The Egyptian Event, they call it. For some reason he thinks I can make news out of it, and his logic, if you can believe this, is that because I hate horses I'll be able to cover it objectively.'

'Well, you can't fault the reasoning.'

'You can never fault John's reasoning. He is always, always right.'

'Do I detect some affection behind the sarcasm!'

His perception pleased her. 'You do. He is my editor, my uncle, and my guardian. Funny . . . I usually hate to admit that. I suppose I'm afraid people will think I had my job handed to me on a silver platter, when I really worked very hard to get it.'

'No one who's read your work would ever doubt that,' he reassured her. 'So you hate horses, eh?'

She nodded and rolled her eyes. 'They're big, and dumb, and dangerous.'

He laughed easily. 'There's usually a runaway or a bucking bronco behind a statement like that. What's your horse horror story?'

She smiled at the deep, clear sound of his laughter. 'He was very big, and I was very small. I had this inane, little-girl fascination for horses, and Uncle John humoured me by taking me to the stables in Central Park. I think he had this vague illusion that I'd become one of those perfect little ladies in those "dahling" riding outfits that canter through the park on Sundays. Anyway, I fell off. Broke my arm.'

'You're kidding. A Central Park stable horse threw you?'

She chuckled derisively. 'I'm not even sure the horse could move. He was standing still at the time, and looked about a hundred years old, but believe me, he had the killer instinct. You could see it in his eyes. I've never been near the despicable creatures since.'

She liked the way his eyes crinkled when he laughed; the easy way he gave in to amusement, without making her feel it was at her expense. Talking to him was so easy, confiding so effortless, that she began to wonder seriously if this Jacob Lancer, whoever he was, *wasn't* the one. Maybe it didn't hit you like a thunderbolt. Maybe it padded in softly, on little cats' feet, like the fog in Frost's poem.

The stories about growing up in John's bachelor brownstone were a slightly tamer version of 'Auntie

Mame', and she shared her childhood happily, warming with the fond memories. Jacob listened attentively, asked questions that would have been intrusive from anyone else, and laughed a great deal. He seemed to enjoy her nostalgia as much as she did, and by the time the huge jet had taxied to a halt in Cincinnati, she thought he must know more about her history than any man alive, with the single exception of John.

She was oddly delighted to learn he was taking the same puddle-jumper flight to Lexington she was, and chastised him as they changed planes. 'You have a demonic gift for making people talk, you know that?' she said sternly. 'I feel like I've given you my verbal memoirs, and I know absolutely nothing about you.'

He chuckled and covered her hand with his when he saw it tense during take-off. She smiled at the gesture of comfort, and at the consideration of a man perceptive enough to see that she needed it.

'You're a fantastic storyteller, and you've had a fascinating life. Besides, what could be better than picking a reporter's brain? It's supposed to be the other way around, isn't it?'

She blushed until colour brightened her fair cheeks. 'Okay. Party's over. Your turn now. And there really is one question I've wanted to ask since we met. Your physical appearance, right down to the tan, says that you work outside, and that you use your body in your work. It's probably a terrible prejudice, but I would have pegged you for a construction worker. And in what's an even worse prejudice, I've always assumed that the average construction worker is not usually as obviously well-read, articulate, and—well, urbane as you are. Nothing about you, except for your appearance, suggests anything less than a highly educated world traveller. But you don't keep a body in condition like that locked in a library, or on planes.'

He looked at her with mild surprise. 'I think you're the

first woman I've ever met who could make reference to a man's body, let alone admit to him she had evaluated it, without at least a pretence of modest embarrassment.'

'Must come from being raised by a bachelor uncle. There was no one to teach me all those ladylike affectations. But you're evading the question. What is it you do that accounts for the contradiction?'

'Shame on you,' he scolded. 'You've assumed that a blue-collar worker can't be well-read, and that an educated man can't keep in shape. I think you've slandered both groups in one fell swoop.'

'Guilty,' she confessed, 'and I've already said it was prejudiced, and you're still avoiding the question. What do you do for a living?'

He turned the full intensity of his remarkable eyes on her, and smiled sheepishly. 'I train horses not to break the arms of little girls.'

'Be serious.'

'I *am* serious. I'm a horse trainer.'

'Like in a circus?'

His hearty laugh filled the cabin of the small plane. 'Sometimes I wonder, but no, not the way you mean. I train horses for affairs like the Egyptian Event.'

She grimaced involuntarily, recalling her earlier remarks. 'You mean people do that for a living?'

'For a very good living, I'd say. You really *don't* know anything about this business, do you?'

She shook her head with a rueful smile. 'To tell you the truth, I assumed I'd be spending four days with hayseeds in straw hats who ran horses around empty oil drums. Not a very accurate description of you, was it?'

Jacob turned to face her, his eyes dancing. 'It's a very accurate description of what I was at one time, actually. But you're right; I'm moving in a different circle now.' He frowned suddenly, and when he spoke again his voice was low and quiet, as if he were speaking to himself. 'You know, at one time the Arabian horse was more a backyard pet than anything else, the one family horse that could do almost anything—jumping, endurance, racing. And that really wasn't so many years ago. But now . . . well, there's more wealth and power and glamour tied to this business than anyone would have believed twenty years ago. I've haven't decided whether it's a good thing or not. Or whether I belong in it or not. Sometimes I think I'd be more comfortable racing around oil drums in a battered straw hat than doing what I do now.' He smiled suddenly and cocked his head. 'Maybe your editor was right. Maybe an objective viewpoint *will* make a better story. And if outsiders still see us as a group of illiterate cow punchers, an outsider's honest report might do the Arabian industry a world of good.'

Valerie frowned, sensing a good deal more to Jacob Lancer than what showed on the surface. 'It would seem I have a lot to learn,' she admitted. 'Any chance of talking you into some tutoring over the next few days?'

He smiled slowly, deep dimples indenting the smooth bronze of his cheeks. 'If it will mean spending time with you, I'm yours whenever I'm not working.' There was a promising invitation in his eyes, and Valerie returned his gaze with a curious smile, thinking that if the plane didn't crash, and if a horse didn't trample her, this assignment might not be so bad after all.

CHAPTER TWO

SHE was surprised to see a small throng of people waiting for them inside the tiny, crisply modern terminal. Cameras clicked in rapid, staccato succession and hands armed with microphones attached to portable tape recorders were thrust rudely past her to bob in front of Jacob's face. The questions from a dozen different voices piled on top of one another until sorting them out became impossible. For the first time, Valerie realised that, in his business at least, Jacob was a celebrity. It was a little disconcerting to be on the other side of a group of persistent reporters, and she wondered if she often appeared as pushy and as rude as these people appeared to her.

'Mr Lancer! Are you bidding for Rissom, or yourself?'

'Is it true you're leaving Rissom, Jacob?'

'Will you make a statement about syndicating Sheikh el Din?'

His tall, blond good looks seemed suddenly polished, and Valerie caught an unpleasant glimpse of the public Jacob Lancer, quite different from the casual, unassuming man she had grown to like so well.

Jacob's voice rose above the din with good-natured authority. 'Ladies! Gentlemen! Please! We have four days for this. I'll be available for the press at the Rissom stalls tomorrow morning at eight. I'll answer all your questions then. Right now all I can think of is how to persuade this ravishing young woman to have dinner with me. Horses—even straight Egyptian Arabian horses—have to take second place occasionally.'

He smiled conspiratorially and held up a hand to halt the rush of questions that followed. 'You all know how dearly I love and protect my social life, or at least you profess to in print.'

There was an almost bawdy, laughing response.

'So you know better than to ask any questions about my lovely companion.' He put an arm casually around Valerie's shoulder, and for some inexplicable reason, the gesture, performed easily in front of a crowd of strangers, made her feel tainted. She tensed under his arm.

'I expect to see most of you tomorrow morning,' he continued, 'but you'll have to excuse us now. The trip was really very tiring.'

He pushed Valerie gently but firmly through the parting line of curious eyes, focused on her with more attention that she thought was warranted. Only when they were safely alone in a taxi outside the terminal did he seem to relax, to revert to the open, honest man she had found so appealing on the plane.

'Sorry about that,' he said, running a hand back through his thick, light hair. 'I should have anticipated that group, and warned you ahead of time. Someone must have leaked my flight schedule. I thought we'd have more time to plan this together.'

She questioned him suspiciously. 'Plan what?'

He pressed his lips together nervously. 'Look. If these people find out who you are, you aren't going to get a straight answer out of any of them. They'll just tell you what they want to see in print. We get enough of that kind of reporting from the horse publications. It's high time an objective source took a good, hard look at the Arabian industry.' He moved his eyes sideways to glance at her, guilt across his face like a curtain. 'I just thought a cover might help out—so they didn't start asking who you were when you started asking questions.'

Valerie turned sideways and leaned back against the car door, realisation dawning in her face. 'Let me get this straight,' she began, irritation creeping into her voice.

'You're a real celebrity in this business, aren't you?'

He nodded. 'I'm disgustingly famous.'

Her mouth registered disapproval. 'And a notorious playboy, I gather.'

'If you believe what you read,' he admitted reluctantly.

'And you just implied to the media that I'm your—your "companion" for the duration. One in a long line, I would guess—and *that's* my cover?'

He turned to face her sheepishly. 'It was out of line. I'm sorry.' His eyes narrowed, regarding her intently. 'Is it really that repulsive? Being linked with me?'

She sighed and turned to face the front of the car. 'I'm not sure. Frankly, you seem very different on the ground. I think I liked you better airborne.'

'When you were the public figure, and not me?'

'What's that supposed to mean?' she snapped.

'Maybe Valerie Kipper doesn't like playing second fiddle to a horse trainer.'

Her dark eyes were as steady and level as her voice. 'Valerie Kipper doesn't like playing some man's woman,' she emphasised the last word contemptuously. 'It has nothing to do with playing second fiddle, as you call it.'

His face was boyishly earnest once again, his eyes apologetic. 'All right. I understand. It offends your liberal sensibilities. I should have known better than to pull a stunt like that with a woman like you. At least it can be easily rectified. I'll just introduce you formally at the press conference tomorrow morning.' He held an imaginary microphone to his lips and pronounced with great dignity, 'And now, ladies and gentlemen, may I introduce Valerie Kipper, renowned investigative journalist, here to do an in-depth report on the Arabian horse industry. Please be absolutely natural, and absolutely honest, so she can print the truth about us in the *American Bulletin!*'

She drummed her fingers on her arm, trying not to smile. 'You think I'll intimidate them, that they won't be themselves.'

He shrugged. 'That wouldn't be an unheard-of re-action to national news coverage, would it? We all want to put our best foot forward.'

'Okay, okay. So it's not such a bad idea to have a cover,' she said finally, and his sudden grin was so infectious that she burst out laughing. 'Maybe I will get a better insight into this ridiculous business of yours if the players don't know who I am. But honestly, Jacob, that particular cover? I'm not very good at playing quiet, submissive women, and not sure I like the idea of being accepted as one. How will you ever convince anyone that's what I am?'

'Sorry about choosing that particular disguise,' he answered with a mischievous lift of one brow. 'It was the only thing I could think of at the time. And as far as convincing the masses, it's already done. After the airport, the entire Arabian community will already have assumed that Jacob Lancer is courting . . . again. By tomorrow morning, almost everyone here will know that you're my mistress.'

But he was wrong. It didn't take that long.

CHAPTER THREE

IT was simple coincidence that she and Jacob were registered at the same motel, but his smug satisfaction made it seem like more. He made a great show of escorting her about the facilities in a brazen, possessive manner she resented deeply, and only redeemed himself by recognising that she was offended, and apologising quietly as he escorted her to her room. She promised to meet him in the dining room for dinner, and escaped gratefully to the privacy of her room.

It was easy to sink up to her neck in the steaming water of the bath, to allow the heat to relax the right shoulder muscle that always tightened first under tension. She closed her eyes and concentrated on the contradictory feelings that Jacob aroused in her.

He didn't fit into any category her limited experience with men included, but how could he? His profession precluded that. She had never encountered, let alone become involved with, any man whose life revolved around animals. Perhaps that was what made him so different, that, and the obvious wealth he enjoyed from his position. She had already learned that although she liked the private Jacob Lancer very much, the public Jacob Lancer was something else altogether. Now all she had to determine was which one was real, and which the façade.

Even the title 'trainer' was intriguing, and she wondered idly if the standards of his job dictated the standards of his personal relationships. Were his women expected to behave with the same obedience as the animals he trained? It was an interesting, if irritating hypothesis, and she stood in the bath to turn on a spray of cold water, suddenly indignant.

She dressed carefully, purposefully, in a silk jumpsuit almost precisely the shade of Jacob's eyes. The neckline plunged dangerously, as if pointing to the tiny, tightly cinched waist, and the billowing wrist-length sleeves accentuated the natural grace of her arms and hands. She toyed with her hair, finally letting it fall in soft waves around her face, consciously practising all the age-old feminine wiles she normally despised. There would be a great deal of satisfaction in enticing a womaniser, she thought smugly. Let's see if he can handle an animal with more brains than a horse.

He rose slowly from the chair in the lobby as he saw her approach, his eyes frank with admiration. 'This afternoon I thought I would never meet a woman more beautiful that you were,' he said softly, 'but it would seem I have already.'

She automatically checked his eyes to assess the compliment, and found it genuine. 'I was about to accuse you of practising your line,' she smiled, 'but your apparent sincerity is impressive. I'll thank you instead.'

He said nothing, simply stood before her, his hands at his sides and his shoulders thrown back in a posture that was both confident, yet defenceless. His white shirt was open at the neck, a sharp contrast to the dark golden sheek of his skin, and she was uncomfortably aware of the animal magnetism of his healthy good looks, the throatiness of his voice.

'I suppose you've heard all the compliments a million times,' he said. 'They must fall on deaf ears by now. There would be nothing original left for me to say.'

'That was,' she said softly, then took a step closer and lifted her eyes to his, testing her own reaction to the proximity of their bodies.

He was unusually silent as they ordered cocktails, and eyed her speculatively over the rim of his glass after they had been served. His gaze was too penetrating, the silence too pervasive.

'What a lovely dining room,' she said finally, struggling to re-establish the same easy companionship they had had on the plane. But now she was faced with yet another Jacob Lancer, this one silent and brooding, and obviously uncomfortable. 'Is it something I said?' she asked.

'I'm sorry. I haven't won any awards for brilliant conversation yet this evening, have I?' he said at last. His brief smile was totally without confidence. 'I hate to admit it, I hate the feeling. I'm intimidated. That's all there is to it. I've never felt that way with a woman before, and I don't know quite how to handle it.'

She tried to keep the disappointment out of her voice. So he wasn't the one. Could never be the one. 'Why intimidated?' she asked.

He shrugged in exasperation. 'Oh, I wish you could see me operate. No, on second thoughts, I don't wish that at all. It's just that normally I'm so comfortable with women, so confident. But with you . . . I don't know.' He sighed in frustration. 'Intelligence must give beauty a dimension I never dreamed existed. Or maybe I never encountered it before. But you take my breath away.'

The confession was so simple, so earnest, that she softened immediately, regretting her private conviction to shatter this man's composure. Her hand covered his in a sisterly kind of assurance. He sensed the difference in her touch, and his fingers stiffened under hers. 'Never mind, Jacob. No one else will see that. But for Heaven's sake, relax. Humility is totally out of character for you. Swaggering seems more your style. Just pretend I'm another one of your regulars.'

He looked at her sadly. 'Not a chance,' he whispered. 'Not a chance.'

CHAPTER FOUR

JACOB excused himself to retrieve something from his room, and she leaned back in the padded chair, relaxing for the first time. She lifted her arms to rest on the semicircle of the chair's low back and tipped her head to relieve the tension crick in her neck. Her hair tumbled down her back and away from her face in a soft cascade of colour, and she closed her eyes briefly.

'Very pretty.' The voice came from behind her and to her left, and she looked over her shoulder and up into the dark, humourless face of a man who looked vaguely familiar.

'So you're Jacob's new conquest,' the man said with admiring indifference. 'I must say he's outdone himself this time.'

He walked around to stand across the table in front of her, and she straightened quickly, her cheeks hot with indignation. She caught her lower lip between her teeth to stop the automatic denial, and took a deep breath to calm herself. His eyes dropped frankly to the swell of her breasts rising above the plunging neckline, and she berated herself silently for setting herself up for such rude appraisal. Her hands clenched into fists in her lap, and her eyes flashed.

'I assume you're a friend of Jacob's, and that you inspect livestock for a living,' she said sharply.

She wasn't prepared for the harsh sound of his laughter, as if it were a verbal excess he didn't perform often.

His straight, black brows arched slightly. 'Perhaps I've underestimated Jacob—and you, although I doubt it. A woman who dresses like that,' he inclined a strong, square chin to her neckline, 'is usually asking for inspection.'

She suppressed a childish urge to bolt for the door as he folded his long body into the chair opposite hers, and covered her uneasiness with a cool stare. 'If you're looking for Jacob, he's gone to his room.'

The man merely nodded, and signalled to the waiter.

His indifference infuriated her, and she felt the hot rush of blood to her neck and cheeks. 'Unless Jacob invited you to join us, you're intruding, and I'd like you to leave,' she said firmly.

He turned slowly to face her, and the impact of his dark eyes was almost electric. 'Jacob is always pleased to see me,' he said simply, then nodded to the approaching waiter who backed away with a comical bow, as if in the presence of royalty.

'We'll see about that,' she snapped, and turned her face away, intensely uncomfortable under his gaze.

She chastised herself for ever agreeing to the charade, and wondered if the resulting story would merit the folly of allowing people like this man to believe she was Jacob's current mistress. She was suddenly totally certain that the title was not flattering, and every fibre of her being rebelled against playing the role. It has better be a damn good story, she thought.

Her discomfort was an alien, unpleasant sensation. She was normally supremely confident in her ability to deal with any situation, and that confidence surrounded her with an air of superiority that usually made those around her uncomfortable, not the other way around.

She forced herself to relax in her chair, to assume the pose, if not the actuality, of command. She intentionally directed her full attention frankly and without embarrassment to the man opposite her.

His face was almost ascetic, the sharp angles of prominent cheekbones making him appear sinister in the shadows of the dining room. He was deeply tanned, like

Jacob, but the golden glow of Jacob's light colouring was
absent in the face that Valerie knew would be naturally
dark without benefit of sun. His eyes were deep brown
and cynical, his hair a heavy thatch of thick black that fell
over one side of his forehead to meet the line of a brow
now raised in amusement.

'Is that what it feels like?' he asked.

'What.'

'To be appraised, like livestock.'

She lifted her shoulders in an elegant shrug.

'Speaking as a man, of course, it's strangely re-
freshing. Women are rarely as frank as that. They
seldom stare. But as a woman who must experience that
sort of appraisal often, I would think you'd tire of it.
Then again, you must enjoy it, or you wouldn't encourage it by dressing like that.'

She clenched her teeth and fought the impulse to slap
his face.

He saw the temptation flicker in her eyes, and smiled.
'Unless my ability to read faces has failed me, there's a
spark of intelligence behind those murderous glances of
yours. How the hell did you ever hook up with Jacob
Lancer? Intelligence has never been a priority in his
selections.'

'You are an intolerably rude man,' she said, struggling
to control her anger. 'Who are you?'

His eyes met hers steadily, and the intensity of his gaze
made her tremble. 'More importantly, who are you? It's
comically obvious that you're not Jacob's usual fare.'

There was a twinge of gratitude to be recognised as
something other than a sexual plaything, and her face
softened slightly. Without warning he reached out,
cupped her chin in his hand, and tipped her face up to
his, exposing the long line of her throat. His eyes
explored her face quickly, and he frowned. She held her
breath, motionless under his touch.

'Charles.' Jacob's voice was tense and controlled as he

appeared suddenly behind them, and she felt a slight tightening of the fingers under her chin. The hand remained where it was for a fraction of a moment, as if to impress both Valerie and Jacob that the owner removed it of his own volition, and no one else's.

Jacob remained standing in an unconscious attempt to retain whatever advantage height might give him. His eyes had darkened to a near navy blue, and his face was flushed.

'Do sit down, Jacob. It's your table after all. And your woman.' The tone of the dark man's voice belied the words, saying clearly that he could have either if he wished, the implied insult being that he didn't want them.

Jacob flinched and took his seat quickly, his eyes darting uneasily to Valerie, trying to assess her reaction. She reassured him with a nervous smile, and he relaxed slightly. 'You've met, then.'

'Not formally, no,' Charles replied, looking at Valerie. 'She looks a bit familiar. I was just trying to place the face. You wouldn't think it could be easily forgotten.'

Jacob covered his hesitation with a long swallow from his drink. 'Valerie,' he said finally, 'please meet Charles . . .'

'Rissom,' the darker man supplied.

The eyes of the two men locked briefly before Jacob continued. 'Charles is my employer,' he explained. 'And this is my friend, Valerie.'

'Valerie Smith,' she inserted after a brief pause, inclining her head slightly.

'Indeed.' Rissom's expression plainly doubted the last name, but he said nothing to question it. 'Well, then, Ms Smith, how long have you and Jacob been . . . friends? I don't remember ever hearing him speak of you.'

She looked directly into his eyes, then realised her mistake. They commanded her complete attention, and made her feel as if she had to defend herself against his scrutiny. She completely forgot what she had intended to say.

'We haven't known each other long,' Jacob put in hastily. 'Valerie's brand new to the Arabian business. The Egyptian Event will be a learning experience of sorts.'

Charles nodded soberly. 'I see. Then we should all work to make her feel welcome, to help her learn as much as possible in the next few days.' He paused to taste the drink the waiter had set before him, then nodded. 'Excellent, Robert. Thank you very much.'

The waiter bobbed in another curiously deferential bow, and slipped away silently.

Rissom opened a menu and offered it to Valerie as if they were alone. 'I recommend the Steak Diane, and the veal. I'm afraid they don't do very well with the seafood.'

She felt his fingertips brush hers as she took the menu, and pulled her hand away quickly, her eyes incredulous at the deliciously frightening warmth that ran quickly from her fingers all the way up to her throat. She scanned the menu, then placed it on the table, acutely aware of his eyes on her, embarrassed by the uncontrollable flush she felt creeping up her neck. Suddenly it was unbearably hot.

'I'll have the capon, I think,' she said quickly. 'Would you order for me, Jacob? I'll be back in just a moment.' She rose gracefully from the table and crossed the dining room with a poise she did not feel.

In the unkind glare of the powder-room lights, she soaked a paper towel in cold water and pressed it to her neck, watching her reflection in a distorted mirror. She was reassured by what she saw, thankful that the nervousness she felt was not evident in the haughty face staring back at her.

She had always been aware that others considered her

beautiful, and the knowledge had made her confident. But for the first time in her life, the scrutiny of a man was making her fearful. It astonished her to realise she was afraid that he would appraise her callously, and in some way find her wanting. For one flashing moment, she wished her eyes were brighter, her nose longer, her cheeks more colourful. Then the frivolity of such childishness struck her, and she shuddered with fury that a man she hardly knew was making her wish she were different simply to be more pleasing to him.

She took several deep breaths, then watched in the mirror as her face paled with the realisation. This was the one. She did not doubt it for a moment. Ruthless, cynical, domineering; even with all of this, he was the one.

Her mind fluttered in confusion, hopping from one thought to the next, then she nodded to her reflection, suddenly calm with the knowledge of what she would do. She would return to the dining room and tell him the truth; expose herself as the journalist she was, refute her cover as Jacob's mistress, and apologise for the deception. She could not, would not drive this man away. She might lose a story, but suddenly that seemed a very trivial matter indeed.

She approached the table uncertainly, her mind reeling with emotions she had never hoped to experience, her eyes locked on the back of Rissom's head. She was giddy with anticipation, afraid of rejection, and childishly hopeful as one who finally sees light at the end of a very long tunnel. The name clicked suddenly, unexpectedly, in her brain, and she nearly stumbled. Charles Rissom. *The* Charles Rissom? Surely not—and yet it must be! She slipped immediately into professionalism as she mentally tabulated what little was known about him.

The last of America's great entrepreneurs; those magnificent, fabulously wealthy self-made men who clustered and thrived in great numbers in the country's youth, dwindling to a pathetic few as the century wore on. Charles Rissom was a giant, even among giants.

His conglomerate absorbed corporations like a hungry amoeba, spitting out those he found wanting, leaving millionaires in the wake of his passing through those companies he retained and nourished. He hated the press, and had never in the brief course of his meteoric rise to untold wealth and power, been interviewed. In fact, the only known photograph of Rissom, Valerie recalled with a rueful twist of her mouth, was a grainy, blurred telephoto shot of him riding an Arabian horse, taken years before.

Her reporter's instinct clashed sharply with the emotions this man had aroused in her, and her head ached with the conflict. Tell the truth, and sacrifice the greatest piece of investigative journalism she might ever do? Or maintain the charade as Jacob's mistress, the perfect cover to interview Rissom without his knowledge, and thereby assure his disdain?

The choice was too painful to face squarely, and she slid uncertainly into her chair as both men rose politely.

CHAPTER FIVE

CHARLES had lit a cigarette in her absence, and contemplated her silently through a wreath of smoke. She felt his eyes on her, but could not look at him. Not yet.

'You seem to be lost in thought, Ms Smith.'

She had to face him now. She had to look into those eyes. She had to make a decision.

'Anticipating the night ahead with Jacob, perhaps?'

The words cut deeply, shattering one illusion, replacing it with determination. She was almost grateful to him. The decision had been taken from her hands.

Throughout the course of the meal, she allowed her eyes to rest on Jacob's face in bright attention as he spoke, lingering a fraction of a second longer than necessary. When she spoke to him, she inclined her body ever so slightly in his direction, and smiled in satisfaction to note Rissom's frowning thoughtfulness, his meticulous attention to the nuances of her body language. There was a constant throb of regret that she was convincing Rissom she was not available to him, but his cool distance was a painful reminder that as Jacob's woman, she did not interest him, and she smothered her regret quickly each time it arose.

If Jacob suspected the calculated purpose of her sudden attention to him, he gave no outward sign. If anything, he seemed dazzled by her responses, and exuded a boyish, eager charm she found slightly out of character. She thought Rissom sensed it too, and caught an occasional glimpse of a face dark with disapproval when she paid particular attention to Jacob.

'I really didn't expect to see you until Saturday, Charles,' Jacob remarked at one point. 'Normally you trust me to do the preliminary evaluation of horses you're interested in before a sale.'

Rissom's smile was almost indulgent. 'Don't be paranoid, Jacob. I still do. I just finished my business in Chicago early, and wanted to get the taste of that city out of my mouth. Besides, I haven't been to an Arabian function since Scottsdale. This is supposed to be my relaxation, and it's a long time from February to June.'

'Scottsdale Week is in February,' Jacob explained to Valerie. 'It's one of the highlights of our year in this industry. Several auctions, one of our most prestigious shows, and the chance to start or close any number of business deals.'

Valerie nodded with pretended interest. 'I remember seeing something about it on the national news at the time. As I recall, horses on the block there often sold for six-figures and up. It sounded like big business to me. Million dollar deals are your relaxation, Mr Rissom?' She turned politely to face him, and only quivered slightly when his eyes locked on hers, so great was her control.

'A businessman never totally escapes business, Ms Smith. One tends to manage one's hobbies with the same devotion, until they become businesses in themselves.'

'So Arabian horses were originally just a hobby with you?'

There was a long, uncomfortable silence as he studied her face with a curious frown, as if he were debating whether or not to answer her question. She felt as if her identity and her purpose were written across her forehead in large bright letters. 'This woman has deceived you. She is a reporter. She will invade your privacy, then print it for all the world to read.' She sighed with relief when he finally spoke.

'It was a hobby for a time. Unfortunately, the challenge of "making it" in the industry was too tempting.

And frankly, there was a great deal of money to be made. It's difficult to allow sentimental attachment for an animal to prevail when he's worth upwards of a million dollars. So the hobby became a business quickly, and now my operation is too vast to be termed relaxation. Sometimes I wish I had ignored the investment opportunities altogether.'

There was genuine regret in his voice, and it was the first sincere emotion Valerie had detected since meeting him. She sensed a deep emotional barrier between the man presented to outsiders, and the private Charles Rissom. This was the story she was looking for.

'I don't think I've ever heard anyone regret success so sincerely,' she said. Jacob laughed, and encouraged by her attention, placed a hand over hers possessively. She had to concentrate not to pull her hand away.

'She's got your number already,' he told Rissom with a lopsided smile. 'Charles here,' he continued, 'is the modern day King Midas. Everything he touches seems to turn to gold. Even those things he would love to keep for himself, out of the public eye. He's an extremely jealous man, you know.'

Valerie saw Rissom's eyes flicker with astonishment at Jacob's perception.

'Not the man-woman type of jealousy, of course,' Jacob went on, daring after his second glass of wine. 'He's above attachments of that sort, unlike the rest of us peasants. Too petty, too mundane for Charles. But with his possessions, he's maniacally private. Selfish, in fact. Do you know he has horses worth a fortune locked away in his barn? Horses so valuable they could have tremendous impact on the Arabian breed, and he keeps them hidden away, out of sight, just for his own pleasure.'

'They're mine,' Rissom said suddenly, his voice dangerously low.

Jacob was oblivious to the threatening tone. 'Trouble

is, they become too valuable, and the businessman in Charles finally wins out over the sentimentalist. Then he gives them to me to promote, and ends up hating himself for letting them go. He's disturbed this year because I took his favourite stallion from his godforsaken hideaway in Minnesota, and made him a national champion. You'll see him here tomorrow.'

Valerie's mind leaped. 'Minnesota?'

Jacob shook his head in what he assumed was shared disbelief. 'Almost beyond imagining, isn't it? Retreating to a state where the winters kill anyone born south of the Mason-Dixon line. But it's paradise to Charles.'

'It's private,' Charles said pointedly, and Jacob was immediately silenced.

Valerie realised that the location of Rissom's private estate had probably been the best-kept secret in media history until this moment, and spoke quickly to cover any visible sign of her interest.

'Tell me about the stallion,' she prompted Rissom. 'What makes him so special?'

Jacob jumped in eagerly, unable to remain silent when his favourite subject was the topic of conversation. 'He's probably the greatest straight Egyptian Arabian stallion since Nazeer—he was the foundation for some of today's best—and Sheikh will enjoy the same reverence in years to come. He's the beginning of a dynasty.'

Jacob's voice had deepened with a reverence Valerie found amazing. How could anyone become so obsessed with a horse?

'And Mr Rissom had him hidden away in . . . Minnesota, was it?'

'Jabob feels I was keeping the horse from his destiny,' Charles interjected drily.

'And were you?' she asked, intrigued by the depth of feeling in Rissom's voice; a quiet, deeper feeling, markedly different from Jacob's ebullience.

'I suppose so. Sheikh was never a legend to me, which

is how Jacob sees him. He was a friend.' His words were simple and final, as if the horse were dead.

'I'd like to meet him,' she said without thinking, and wondered immediately why she had said something so inane. She had spoken as if the horse were a person, instead of a dumb animal. And why would she want to 'meet' him anyway? She hated the filthy creatures, one and all.

Rissom's dark eyes lightened momentarily as he searched her face, then he looked down at his plate. 'I'm sure Jacob will be showing him to the press in the morning. You can see him at his best then.' He raised his head quickly and focused his attention on Jacob. 'Speaking of which, Jake,' he used the shortened name almost fondly, 'you'll have a very early morning tomorrow to prepare for the press conference. If you'd like to excuse yourself now, I'll be happy to see Ms Smith to her room.'

Jacob's eyes flashed suspiciously across the table, then lowered as he crumpled his napkin and tossed it on the table. 'You're right, of course. Tomorrow will be the worst day of the four. Valerie, forgive me, but I'm here to do a job first, although for the first time in my life, I'm finding the company of a woman more interesting than that of a horse.'

Charles raised his eyebrows in surprise, and Valerie laughed graciously. As little as she knew of Jacob, she was certain that being accorded a slot above horses was rare praise indeed. 'Good night, Jacob,' she said warmly, taking his hand in hers. He returned the pressure of her fingers almost desperately before turning reluctantly to leave. She intentionally followed him with her eyes until he left the dining room, then moved in her chair to face Rissom squarely. His eyes were on her in curious contemplation.

'You're staring, Mr Rissom.'

His lips twisted into a wry smile. 'My compliments, Ms

Smith. I've seen Jacob through countless women, but this is the first time the poor man has ever been hopelessly infatuated himself. It'll go hard with him. I don't think he ever believed in love before now.'

She was immediately on the defensive, guarding her cover story. 'What makes you think it will go hard on him, Mr Rissom?'

'Because, Ms Smith, for all your very convincing pretence, I don't believe a woman like you has the slightest intention of becoming permanently involved with a man like Jacob, whatever your sexual relationship. What puzzles me is what possible benefit you could gain from milking the poor fellow.'

She bristled automatically, but forced herself to sit quietly, to continue playing the role. 'I'm very fond of Jacob,' she protested, 'and you speak of him as if he were a child, when you must be very close to his age yourself.'

'We're the same age, in fact. We're both thirty.'

'Thirty,' she mused alound. 'That's very young to be so cynical.'

'I could say the same of you, I think.' He raised his hand slightly without taking his eyes from hers, and the waiter appeared immediately at his elbow.

'The usual, sir?'

'Please, Robert. Perhaps Ms Smith will join me. A small after-dinner drink,' he explained. 'A recipe of my own, which Robert prepares beautifully.'

She inclined her head and Robert hustled away in obvious delight to be of service.

'Now then, Ms Smith,' he began, 'I think it's time you told me the truth.' His eyes were fastened on hers, and she felt her pulse quicken.

'The truth about what, Mr Rissom?' she asked coolly.

He hesitated, intentionally she was sure, and she squirmed in her chair, waiting for him to demand to know her real identity, to expose her as a fraud. She was so emotionally taut by the time he finally spoke that the question seemed ridiculously anti-climatic.

'How is it that a woman with your obvious attributes remains unmarried? Or at least I assume you're unmarried.' He smiled coldly at the flash in her eyes.

'One might ask the same question of you, Mr Rissom,' she shot back.

His brows arched and he smiled in feigned surprise. 'Are you flattering me, Ms Smith? Does that mean you find me attractive? A subject worthy of matrimonial consideration?'

He was mocking her deliberately, and she struggled to remain calm, fighting the impulse to end the conversation and storm from the room. 'You have a certain appeal, I suppose,' she conceded with a biting edge to her voice. 'Not universal, mind you, but a sort of ruthless, animal vitality that might intrigue a certain type of woman.'

His smile broadened. 'And what type of woman might that be?'

'A masochist,' she answered without hesitation, and his laugh filled the room.

'You've been trying so hard not to say things you've wanted to say to me all evening, Ms Smith. I'm glad you finally slipped. Even honest revulsion is better than the polite, cold mask you've been wearing. I like you better this way. Ah, thank you, Robert. Here, Valerie.'

She frowned at his unexpected use of her given name, perplexed at his apparent delight with what she had hoped would be a biting insult. 'What is it?' She accepted the long-stemmed goblet and sniffed the frothy cream contents suspiciously.

'A little bit of many intriguing things, much like yourself.'

When genuine, his smile was beautifully contagious, and she smiled helplessly in response, touching her glass to his.

CHAPTER SIX

SHE could not remember afterward when she began calling him Charles instead of Mr Rissom. Nor could she recall unconsciously shedding the pretence of being Jacob's mistress, or the role of journalist. She asked many questions, and absorbed the answers dutifully, but a sincere interest in the man had prompted them, not a reporter's curiosity.

He responded in kind, and what began as a light, bantering exchange of two cynics trying to out-do one another soon developed into a warm, intimate conversation. His caustic sarcasm had disappeared like a mask he had tossed aside in the company of friends, and she felt totally isolated in a small world existing only for the moment, taking simple pleasure from his company.

She explored the intricacies of his mind through two of the slightly intoxicating, dangerously delicious drinks he called 'ADs'.

'Is that for After Death?' she had asked.

'After Dinner,' he had replied, laughing easily.

The two hours they lingered at the table were a magical retreat from reality, and it was only when they rose to leave the dining room that the illusion crumbled, and she remembered her purpose. Sadness crossed her face in a childishly visible wave, and Charles instinctively grasped her hand and pressed it to his cheek. 'What is it, Valerie?'

She shook her head slowly, her eyes liquid and sorrowful. 'I forgot,' she said simply. 'I totally forgot.'

He frowned and led her from the dining room into the relative quiet of the corridor, where he turned her gently to face him. 'Forgot what?'

She trembled under the touch of his hands, and shrugged helplessly. 'Why I was here,' she answered.

She knew he would assume she was referring to her relationship with Jacob, and struggled not to blurt out that it was all a lie, that she was his for the asking. If his face had fallen, if he had only shown a trace of tenderness, of disappointment, she might have done just that. Instead, his eyes narrowed and his jaw clenched until his mouth was a bitter line.

'Jacob,' he said harshly, and his fingers tightened on her shoulders.

She winced under the pressure, and took a step backwards.

He dropped his hands abruptly, discarding her, and she felt suddenly empty, apathetic.

She expected him to turn and walk away, and started with surprise when he grabbed her arm and jerked her roughly towards him. 'What room are you in?'

'One . . . one ninety-seven,' she stammered, 'but it's not necessary for you to . . .'

'Nonsense. I told Jacob I'd see you to your room, and I will. What I don't understand is why your room is so far from his. He always stays close to the lobby. Damned inconvenient, isn't it? Trotting so far from one room to another in the middle of the night? Or don't you even pretend to keep up appearances?'

She tugged at her arm with a vicious jerk, but his fingers only tightened around it. 'The pretence of offence is a little silly at this late date, don't you think, Ms Smith? You are, after all, Jacob's mistress, and made no attempt to pretend otherwise, although we both seemed to forget it for a time. How fortunate for Jacob that you finally remembered.'

He moved down the hall, nearly dragging her along, and she took faster and faster steps, feeling miserably like a child subjected to an adult pace. He released her arm at the door to her room, and she reached up unconsciously to rub it.

'Give me your key,' he demanded.

She straightened to her full height and clutched her dinner bag tightly, her face white and pinched. 'I'll open my own door,' she said slowly, 'after you leave.'

He snatched the bag from her hands, retrieved the key, then opened the door and pushed her roughly inside, tossing her bag on to the bed.

'There,' he said deliberately. 'I've seen you to your room, as promised. Good night, Ms Smith.' His face was pale and drawn, bitter lines pulling down at the corners of his mouth.

An instinctive rage at being treated so shabbily, and a deep sorrow at losing the warm, gentle companion of just a few moments before, pulled an emotional drawstring, and Valerie hiccoughed in a furious attempt not to cry. One tear escaped her vigil and traced a delicate, curving line down her cheek, catching and reflecting the dim light from the hall.

Rissom hesitated as he turned, closing his eyes briefly as if he were in pain. Then he reached out and touched her cheek gently, smoothing away the glistening drop with his thumb, frowning in confusion. The tenderness of the gesture cracked Valerie's control completely, and the tears came unbidden as she stood before him stiffly, her head thrown back, her eyes closed, not caring that she was leaving herself open to his ridicule. She felt his hand leave her face, then heard his heavy step to the door, followed by the quiet click of the latch as it closed. Her chin dropped to her chest, her eyes still closed, and her small shoulders slumped.

'Damn!' she whispered. 'Damn! Damn!'

Her eyes flew open as heavy hands grasped her shoulders, and she looked up into eyes nearly black with emotion. His lips parted to show a flash of white as he lowered his face with tortuous slowness, his breath coming in short, hard gasps that came faster and faster as his lips drew near. He pulled her body close to his while holding his head inches away, and commanded her with his eyes. A violent surge of heat coursed upward from her legs through her stomach to her throat, releasing in a shudder of anticipation as she waited for their lips to meet. His mouth was nearly touching hers, his breath hot and fragrant on her face as she quivered under him, when he finally closed his eyes and jerked her towards him, crushing her mouth under his. A low moan escaped her lips as his mouth moved down to her neck, his tongue tracing a hot line to the hollow of his throat, down her chest to the gentle swell of her breast. She felt his arm beneath her knees as he lifted her effortlessly and carried her to the bed, and lightning thoughts of her story, her pretended relationship to Jacob, and her long-standing reserve with men evaporated when his hand descended to the buttons on her blouse. She lay still as he jerked open the fragile silk, her eyes wide and alert to the emotions crossing his darkened face, her breasts rising and falling rapidly as she struggled to pull in air.

He straightened suddenly and stood erect next to the bed, his eyes narrow slits in a face twisted with desire. He reached out, his arm stiff from the shoulder, his forefinger burning as it moved from her neck down to her exposed breast. As it brushed lightly against the nipple he gasped sharply, threw his head back and pulled his hand away.

She trembled as she watched the struggle on his face, the rapid pulse at the base of his throat, willing him to take her as she had always longed to be taken without fully realising it; knowing that whatever the consequences, if she could have just this one night with this one man, she would not ask for anything more, ever.

His eyes were squeezed shut, his palms open, and she sensed the battle he was waging with himself, wondering if his strength of will would overcome the demands of his body.

His fingers finally relaxed, his chin dropped, and he opened his eyes to survey her body with an impassive, cursory glance. His forehead glistened with a sheen of perspiration, but his lips lifted in an unpleasant, sardonic smile.

'So,' he said sarcastically, and the sound of his voice was so distorted she hardly recognised it, 'Jacob's woman can be had.'

Her lips parted in dismay and disbelief, and she was suddenly ashamed to be lying half-naked and submissive beneath his ruthless, indifferent appraisal.

His eyes flickered disdainfully to take in her body once more, then he turned and left the room, closing the door quietly behind him. Her humiliation was total, and she lay motionless for a long time after he left, listening without interest to the late-night sounds of the motel.

CHAPTER SEVEN

HE didn't want her. It was as simple as that. She awakened to that thought the next morning, and the shameful memory refused to be erased. For the first time in her life, she had offered all she had to give to the man her heart had chosen, but her heart had been wrong, misled by all those childish notions of love at first sight and happy endings. He had only used her in a cruel game of one-upmanship with Jacob. She shuddered, remembering the disdain in his voice when he noted that 'Jacob's woman can be had.' Jacob took his horse; he took Jacob's woman. Tie score.

She glared into the mirror, hating her role as unwitting pawn in the games men played; hating the men who played such games; hating Charles Rissom for shattering her dreams. The hate became obsessive, and lifted the lingering cloud of disappointment and self-pity from the face she watched in the mirror. Like Uncle John had always said, she was a survivor. And she would survive this. If she couldn't have Charles Rissom, she would at least have his story. He used her, so she would use him. It was only fair. And when all was said and done, she would take from him something equal in value to the pride and the dream he had stripped from her: his privacy.

Her mouth tightened with resolve as she pulled her hair back with a wide ribbon and slipped into a demure, snowy sundress. It pleased her sense of irony that Rissom would see her dressed in pristine white, and she nodded at her reflection, coldly satisfied with the woman who nodded back.

41

She climbed into the hot little box the rental car agency had delivered that morning, and stabbed frantically at the air conditioner controls. Even at eight o'clock in the morning, June was oppressively hot and humid in Kentucky.

She smiled in grim satisfaction as she drove, anticipating Rissom's outrage to see himself in print at last, and to know that a woman he had scorned was responsible. She laughed gently at herself when she realised that that was precisely the role she was playing—a woman scorned—then cringed involuntarily. It was an unfamiliar role, and she hated it.

She passed several large horse farms en route, and marvelled at the endless acres of rolling, lush pasture, enclosed in dazzling white board fences that stretched as far as she could see. The grounds were meticulously cared for, and she shook her head in disgust that such expense should be wasted on horses. It was excessive, it was beyond reason and, recalling that this was one of Charles Rissom's pet ventures, she belittled it with a new intensity that surprised even her. She checked her emotions quickly, realising that her bitterness would seriously jeopardise the effectiveness of her writing. She made a mental promise to exercise total objectivity. That the article would be written at all would be vengeance enough.

Valerie followed the long, winding road to the entrance of the Kentucky Horse Park, suitably impressed with the beauty of the tree-studded grounds and the low, modern building, but irritated anew when she remembered that all of this was yet another monument to the horse. She had yet to understand man's senseless attachment to the animals, and wondered if she would be able to conceal her distaste for the world she was entering long enough to complete her task.

She parked the car and stepped out of the cool, air-conditioned interior, and the sweltering heat of the morning pressed against her, making it difficult to breathe.

She gathered all the literature available in the large information building, and sat on a long wooden bench to read briefly on the origins of The Egyptian Event, and the straight Egyptian Arabian horse, to which it paid homage. After a moment's cursory inspection, she tucked all of the information into her voluminous handbag, deciding to do her homework that evening in her room. The horses, after all, were no longer her primary story—only background as they might relate to Charles Rissom.

She left the building's pleasant coolness for the heat outside, and began a slow, arduous climb up the walk which led to the highest point in the park, upon which stood a large, white barn referred to in the brochures as the 'Hall of Stallions'. Within this structure, she had read, were housed fifty-one of the most valuable horses in the world, and Rissom's would be among them.

The park was nearly deserted at this early hour, and quite pleasant in spite of the oppressive heat. The full force of the sun had yet to inflict its punishment, and the tree-shaded walk wound its way through various exhibits she found mildly interesting, especially the Egyptian booths displaying various *objets d'art* and a dazzling array of brightly coloured, bejewelled costumes. She wondered what possible connection such gaudy, voluminous garb could have with a horse show, and decided to make enquiries later. She paused briefly at the large, open end of the barn, wishing she had worn jeans and flat sandals, or something more in keeping with barn attire, and then entered.

She was immediately grateful for the snobbish instinct that had prompted her to dress in something suitable for a late afternoon stroll on Park Avenue, and wondered perhaps if she weren't slightly underdressed.

Only an occasional nicker or the sudden, muffled thud of a hoof snapping down on heavy bedding gave any indication that the building was a barn at all. At first glance, as soon as her eyes adjusted to the cool, dim interior, it looked like a gaily decorated, spacious pavilion of some sort, holding its breath in sparkling readiness before a gala celebration.

A temporary carpet of subdued royal blue extended the length and breadth of a wide centre aisle. Spotlessly white twists of cotton rope, draped between polished, squat brass posts cordoned off the two narrow aisles on either side, both of which were deep in fresh, sweet-smelling sawdust. What Valerie presumed to be the stalls were completely covered with every fabric imaginable; from gauze to tapestry, to silk she immediately recognised as genuine, in varying shades of the same blue as the carpet. Although the stall decorations were imaginatively different as she passed from one breeder's stall to the next, the consistent theme of the common colour pulled the differences together in a peculiar, subdued elegance of uniformity, and she was reluctantly impressed.

A small knot of people at the far end of the barn announced the location of the Rissom stalls and the accompanying press conference, and she walked hesitantly in that direction. She felt uncomfortably obvious, walking the full length of the empty blue carpet in her brilliantly white dress, and her timidity infuriated her. She had never felt awkward to be the centre of attention before, but there was a subtle shamefulness in knowing she would be identified as Jacob's mistress; and for all her Fifth Avenue clothes and haughty superiority, she felt like she was on display as a common, if expensive, prostitute.

As she drew closer she could see that the reporters were giving their full attention to Jacob, yet she still felt the uncomfortable sensation of eyes upon her; and then she saw him. He was leaning casually against a stall on the side of the barn opposite Charles; long, lean legs stretched out to brace himself, crossed at the ankle. His arms were folded under his broad chest, his head turned to watch her, tipped to one side. She lifted her chin slightly and returned his stare with equal frankness, stopping quickly when a slow, knowing smile spread across his face, as if to say the dress was no protection, and he remembered all too well what she looked like without it.

She realised with distress that he intended to approach her, and quashed a ridiculous impulse to bolt for the door when he pushed himself away from the wall. But she stood her ground, thinking with a lack of real conviction that she had endured worse to get a story in her career, although at that moment she could imagine little worse than confronting a man who had absolutely no respect for her. Especially this man.

There was a tightness in her chest as she watched him walk towards her, his bearing the unmistakable mark of one used to power, and confident in his ability to exercise it. His shirt was open at the throat, tapering from the broad expanse of his chest to a lean, hard waist, and long, muscular legs strode purposefully towards her. His dark eyes glittered as they fastened on hers, but his smile was surprisingly pleasant, and she watched him nervously, waiting to take her cue on how to behave from his first words.

'Good morning, Ms Smith. If anything, you're even more lovely than you were last night.'

Her throat constricted at the deep, melodic sound of his voice, and for a fleeting moment, she felt an almost irrepressible urge to crawl into his arms and confess anything, no matter what the cost. The impulse astounded her, and she shrank from the realisation that she was willing to forgive his rejection, tolerate his arrogance, and ignore her pride—just because the sound of his voice moved her! She had never felt such power from a man, and it frightened her.

But his next words, delivered contemptuously, broke the spell quickly.

'You're much too desirable when you're silent, Ms Smith. You should say something soon, or I may be tempted to rip that very expensive dress from your very expensive body and take you right here, in front of your lover.'

Her mouth dropped open, and her eyes grew wide.

'Oh, come now,' he whispered sarcastically. 'I assure you that if Jacob can afford the price of admission, I certainly can.'

Her arm lifted in a blur on its way to his face, but he captured her wrist easily in his hand and diverted the blow.

'Now, now. Sheath your claws. Jacob has centre stage now, and he dearly loves it. This is neither the time nor the place to show your true colours.'

She gasped in pain as he released her wrist only to grasp her upper arm in the tight circle of his fingers. 'Let go of me!' she hissed, almost spitting with fury, but he merely smiled unpleasantly and pulled her closer to the group of people surrounding Jacob. Since resistance would only have attracted attention, she allowed herself to be led, fighting the childish urge to cry at her helpless captivity.

'Pay attention now,' he whispered as they stopped opposite the Rissom stalls. 'Let Jacob impress you.'

Her muscle tightened under his hand in an effort to release herself unobtrusively, but his fingers pressed cruelly into her flesh, and he jerked her arm slightly, warning her to be still.

'Or what?' she whispered belligerently in answer to the silent threat.

He turned his head to regard her contemptuously. 'Or

what I said I would do, I will do,' he stated without hesitation.

She examined the ruthless set of his jaw, the indifferent contempt of his eyes on hers, and knew with absolute certainty that he meant it. She turned her head stiffly to face front, and focused her attention on Jacob.

There was a peculiar ringing in her ears as she struggled to concentrate on what Jacob was saying. His eyes brushed over hers as he continued to speak to the group, then returned in a double-take of delighted surprise. If anything, he spoke with even more animation, his light head bobbing up and down to accentuate his words. He nodded almost imperceptibly to Charles, and his eyes seemed to darken for a moment, then he focused on Valerie again. She recognised the longing glance of adoration, the puppy-like pleading for acknowledgment, and smiled at him with genuine fondness. His own smile brightened visibly, and he nearly strutted with boyish pleasure.

'You enjoy tormenting him, don't you?' Rissom whispered directly into her ear, and all the hairs on the back of her neck stood up.

She refused to look at him, and denied the accusation to herself in silence. Besides, at the moment, Jacob Lancer was infinitely appealing. His timidity reminded her of other unsatisfactory relationships, it was true. She had drifted aimlessly away from many men who had unconsciously subjugated themselves to her, wondering if she would ever meet a man whose will was stronger than her own, or even if such a man existed. Yet now, captive to just such a man, frustrated by the purely biological accident of his superior strength, Jacob's gentle uncertainty seemed like a safe harbour. She longed to take refuge under the protection of a man capable of dealing with Rissom on a physical level, whether that man was intimidated by her or not. Perhaps she had been wrong all along. Perhaps it was foolish to hope for a relationship with a man who intimidated her, for a change. So far, it was proving only distasteful. She wished desperately that Jacob would finish soon, and rescue her, and looked at him in a new light.

Jacob disappeared briefly into the silk-draped stall behind him, and emerged slowly, leading what looked for all the world to Valerie to be a fire-breathing dragon. She took an involuntary step backward and trembled under Rissom's hand. He looked at her sharply, and saw the fear in her eyes. His fingers tightened on her arm, but more in support than in restraint.

The stallion was almost exactly the colour of Valerie's hair, but with a burnished gloss so dazzling it looked as if he had been sprayed with clear acrylic. The extreme, chiselled features of a surprisingly delicate head were accentuated by enormous, wide-set dark eyes, now rolled back menacingly to show the whites. His nostrils distended to show the vibrant red tissue inside, and his breath came in sharp, furious blows, like a labouring locomotive. His neck was long and muscular, his body rippling with the quiver of a thousand different muscles, and he pranced nervously in place. She could see the distended sinews in Jacob's broad forearm as he held the beast in check.

There was an adamant chorus of admiration from the group of reporters, but Valerie couldn't understand their excitement. She simply thought the horse was terrifying.

Jacob coaxed the beast with sharp cracks from a tiny whip held over his head until the stallion stretched his neck forward, one hind leg extended, and remained at quivering attention while cameras clicked furiously around him.

'He looks like he's going to explode,' Valerie whispered fearfully, her eyes enormous in her pale face.

Rissom's mouth turned up in a lopsided smile, infinitely amused that Jacob had chosen a woman so obviously frightened of horses.

Jacob returned the stallion to his stall, then held up his hands in a what-more-can-I-say gesture.

'One more question, Mr Lancer,' an attractive young woman asked from the front of the group. Her eyes met Jacob's with an invitation Valerie could detect even from a distance, and she wondered if Jacob had that effect on all women. 'Will we ever see Charles Rissom at the Egyptian Event?'

Jacob smiled automatically at the girl, charm exuding from every pore. 'I am quite sure you will—eventually.'

Valerie turned quickly to Rissom, a question in her eyes.

'No,' he answered what she had not yet asked. 'None of them knows who I am. Jacob calls me Charles Smith when introductions are unavoidable, which is why your own last name was less than believable.'

'Just because Smith is a common name doesn't mean it's a false one,' she said, swallowing her guilt. 'Not everyone assumes a fake identity.'

'No. Not everyone. Only those who can't find privacy any other way, and those who wish to deceive.'

'A deception in either case,' she countered.

'I didn't deceive you,' he reminded her. 'I know my name meant nothing to you initially last night, but you made the connection later. You knew who Charles Rissom was.'

'So why did you admit it? Why didn't you introduce yourself as Charles Smith?'

He smiled ruefully. 'I've been asking myself the same question since.' He looked directly into her eyes and she held her breath, powerless under his gaze. 'Let's just say I misjudged you, thought I saw a glimmer of integrity behind those dazzling eyes of yours. Laughable, isn't it, when one remembers how you came to be here?'

The accusation stung, even though it was unde-
served, and she tried to pull her arm from his grasp. He
released it voluntarily as Jacob approached at a jog,
breathless with excitement.

'Valerie! Charles! What did you think? Wasn't he
magnificent?'

'You handled him beautifully, Jake,' Charles flattered
him. 'He's never looked better.'

Jacob flushed with pleasure at the rare praise. 'Why
don't you go into his stall, Charles? You haven't seen
him in almost a year.'

'I just saw him.'

'You know what I mean.' There was a long, uncomfortable pause.

'I know what you mean,' Charles answered finally.
'But another time. I was just keeping Ms Smith company
until you finished. I have an appointment shortly, but I'll
see both of you later.' His eyes rested momentarily on
Valerie's and then he left.

She didn't realise how intently she was watching him
walk away until Jacob's hand turned her chin gently to
face him. He said nothing for a moment as his eyes
searched hers. 'I can't decide if you've fallen in love with
him, or if you're planning to have him killed,' he said
quietly.

She pressed her hand to his and let the barriers fall
away from her eyes, and Jacob's heart turned over to see
her looking so vulnerable. 'You are a perceptive, sensitive man, Jacob. Don't let anyone ever tell you otherwise.'

He chuckled derisively. 'Perceptive, hell. A child
could read your face. Besides, I knew when I left last
night that Charles would move on you. He usually does.
I think it amuses him to test women—especially the
women I'm seeing.' He gaze dropped suddenly. 'And if
he did, it could only have ended in one of two ways.'

She sighed and let her head fall to his shoulder, and his

arms wrapped around her protectively. 'So which is it?' he asked. 'Love, or hate?'

'One would be just as stupid as the other, wouldn't it?'

'Probably.'

'Well then, if they're both equally stupid, I'll opt for hate. It's safer, I think.'

'Come on,' he whispered into her hair. 'I'll buy you a cup of coffee.'

They walked out of the barn, Jacob's arm encircling her shoulders, his head bent towards hers until their hair touched and mingled in a violent contrast of light and dark.

Rissom watched them silently from the dim recess of a side door, his eyes narrowed, his expression dark and terrible.

CHAPTER EIGHT

JACOB stirred his coffee absently, his spoon clinking with irritating regularity against the sides of his cup. He finally lifted it from the steaming liquid and let it fall with a clatter to the table. Valerie started and looked up.

'You haven't said a word since we left the barn,' he admonished her gently.

She smiled and reached out to cover his hand with hers. His eyes flickered at her touch, but she was too preoccupied to notice.

'He didn't know who you were,' he said suddenly, 'or he would never have introduced himself by his real name.'

Her smile faded. 'You're afraid I'll write about him, aren't you Jacob?'

'Don't try to tell me you haven't thought about it.'

'And if I have?'

'I'd stop you, if I could.'

'Why? Because you work for him?'

He shook his head silently.

'You'd protect a man who tries to appropriate your women?' she asked in disbelief.

His shoulders went up to his ears in a helpless shrug.

'Do you like him, Jacob?'

He leaned back in his chair and sighed deeply. 'That's an awkward question. I don't think Charles Rissom is the kind of man you "like". Respect, maybe, even fear—but like?' He rolled his eyes eloquently. 'He's an intensely private man. Cold. Distant. It's hard to like a man like that.'

Valerie smiled in understanding. 'Especially for a man like you.'

'What's that supposed to mean?'

'I think you love everybody who will let you. Charles must frustrate you terribly.'

He grinned, and the confident, boyish charm erased uncertainty from his face. 'Guilty,' he admitted. 'I love 'em all. Even the hateful ones, because they amuse me. Most people do, in fact.' He became suddenly serious, and the periwinkle eyes dazzled her in their earnestness. 'Some more than others, of course. I've only met two people who didn't amuse me at all.'

She frowned. 'Charles Rissom?'

'And you.'

Valerie returned to the motel for lunch, and changed into walking shorts and a cool, loose-fitting camisole. The Kentucky sun had become unmerciful by late morning, and even her sundress had seemed excessive.

She spent her time alone over lunch judiciously, gleaning as much as possible from the brochures she had collected earlier. They were all written with a near reverence for the Arabian horse that baffled her, but she studied the material dutifully, trying to gain some insight into the value of this event's celebrated star: a particular strain of Arabian referred to as the 'straight Egyptian'. She closed the last booklet with a frustrated gesture of finality, understanding less than when she had started, and returned to the park.

The stallion barn was a flurry of activity as owners bathed and groomed their charges, preparing for a spectacle the programme noted as the Parade of Stallions.

Jacob directed a hustling crew of young grooms with quiet authority, managing to remain impeccably aloof from the activity around him. He had changed into dark slacks that hugged his muscular legs and a spotless white shirt with the sleeves rolled up to the elbows, revealing a long expanse of broad, tanned forearm. His light hair shone like a beacon in the barn's dim interior, and when he caught sight of Valerie, the flash of his smile tumbled the heart of every young girl who happened to see it.

His outstretched hands clasped hers warmly. 'Remember when you asked me if I trained horses for the circus?' he asked with a smile. 'Well, days like today make it seem like that's exactly what I'm doing.'

He pulled her quickly out of the way as a prancing stallion was led past them, his shod hooves striking dangerously close to Valerie. She spun away from the flared nostrils and the white-rimmed eyes and pressed against Jacob until the horse was beyond them.

'I'm sorry,' she apologised weakly, pushing away from him. 'I'm really out of my element here. I simply cannot overcome my fear of these animals!'

Jacob wrapped one arm protectively around her shoulders and led her to a side door that opened on a vista of rolling pastureland. 'I need to get out of here myself for a while,' he admitted, pulling her through the doorway. 'The first parade is always the worst—like opening night on Broadway. Everyone has the jitters, and the horses sense it. Tomorrow's will be easier.'

'Tomorrow's? You mean this insanity happens every day?'

He chuckled. 'Every day at 2:00 p.m. All the stallions are taken to the main ring and displayed together. The spectators get a good chance to compare, maybe select the stallion they'll breed their mares to next spring. There isn't another marketplace like it in the industry.'

Valerie shook her head in bafflement, recalling the mental images of activities taking place in the barn behind them: a groom crouched terrifyingly close to nervous, prancing hooves, painting them with what looked like shoe polish, the earnest concentration of a young woman rubbing baby oil into the smooth muzzle of a white stallion until the skin darkened, and the preposterous picture of one placid stallion with eyes closed, nodding into hypnotic slumber while his owner ran an electric razor up and down the insides of his ears.

'Seems like an awful lot of trouble to go through just to lead a horse around a ring,' she murmured.

Jacob laughed heartily. 'The rewards are worth it. We booked twenty-seven mares at last year's event for one of Charles' lesser stallions. We expect better things this year with Sheikh on display.'

'And that makes it all worthwhile?' she asked sceptically.

Jacob's smile was tolerant. 'Sheikh's stud fee is $7,500, Valerie,' he said quietly. 'Multiply that times 30 mares, then you tell me if you think it's worthwhile.'

Valerie's mouth dropped open as she did a rapid mental calculation. 'Jacob!' she whispered. 'That's almost a quarter of a million dollars!'

He nodded solemnly. 'And that's just for 30 mares. We expect to breed at least twice that many next year.'

She rummaged quickly through her purse and pulled out a small notebook with a pen clasped to its cover. Jacob smiled down on her furious scribbling.

'So the journalist is interested at last,' he noted wryly. 'Now do you understand? It isn't just another horse show, Valerie. It's big business.'

She shook her head as she continued writing. 'It's absolutely ridiculous!' she muttered. 'All that money, from *horses*!'

'That's just the tip of the iceberg. Keep your eyes open and your pen out. You'll learn a lot today.'

He sighed deeply and turned back towards the barn reluctantly. 'I have to get back to work, now. How about drinks later, and then dinner?'

She raised her head at the gentle plea in his voice, and saw it reflected in his eyes. 'I suppose we have to,' she smiled. 'If only to keep up appearances.'

He rewarded her with the flashing grin that made him appear so boyish, then frowned suddenly and looked down. 'You may have reason to regret our little charade tonight,' he said hesitantly. 'We're apt to meet a great many people in the restaurant who won't mince words about our . . . relationship.'

Valerie grimaced involuntarily, recalling Rissom's scorn, and Jacob watched her face with a worried frown. 'Charles?' he asked intuitively.

She nodded, then shrugged as if to negate the unpleasant memory. 'I doubt if anyone else could be quite as contemptuous,' she said finally. 'If I made it through Charles Rissom, I can handle anyone.'

Jacob smiled in sympathetic understanding, then looked off at some distant point beyond the horizon. 'I don't know what he said after I left last night, but I know he can be cruel. But some day Charles will go too far,' he said softly, and Valerie thought she detected a veiled threat in his voice. She reached over to lay her hand on his arm, and he looked down at the dainty fingers resting on his sun-darkened skin.

'Valerie?' he whispered wistfully, but he never finished the question. The loudspeaker system over the main ring crackled in to life with a pulsating hum that carried the length and breadth of the park. Jacob came instantly to attention, the muscles in his arm tensing under Valerie's fingers, suddenly oblivious to her touch.

'I have to go now,' he said absently, then his gaze fell on her as if he had just remembered something important.

'Never mind, Jacob.' She turned him away with a gentle push on his shoulder and a laugh full of understanding. 'Your audience is waiting. I'll meet you at the restaurant at six-thirty.'

He shot her a grateful grin and rushed back through the doorway that led to the barn's interior. She watched him retreat with a tolerant smile and a small shake of her head, thinking how very much like a child he was, and how very endearing children could be.

Valerie followed the milling crowd to the sun-baked bleachers on one side of the enormous outdoor ring. She squinted against the glare, silently cursing the heat, the dust, and most of all, the horses responsible for her presence here in the first place. She had been jostled by so many bodies that she paid little attention to the light press of a hand on her back until the fingers traced an intentional line up her spine to the base of her neck. She spun quickly, ready with an indignant retort, then swallowed it when she saw the mocking amusement in the face of Charles Rissom.

'You look delightfully cool,' he remarked, pointedly glancing at the long, slim lines of her legs beneath her shorts.

'Well, I'm not!' she replied irritably, shrugging away from his hand, then wishing immediately that she hadn't. 'I'm hot, and dusty, and tired, and standing out here under that blasted sun to watch a bunch of animals chase each other around in a circle is absolutely insane!' She finished her angry outburst with a deep breath.

'But you suffer through it,' he mocked her, 'for Jacob. How touching.'

She pulled the brim of her hat further down on her forehead with a vicious jerk of her hand, then pushed rudely past the people in front of her in an attempt to leave him behind.

Charles smiled in reluctant appreciation of the body rushing away from him, then quickened his pace to overtake her. 'I can save you from the sun, at least,' he said, grabbing her arm firmly and pulling her back the way she had come.

She stumbled in a useless attempt to resist, and her sandal filled with hot sand. 'Just a minute!' she cried impatiently, feeling the sudden frustration of a small child being dragged along at an adult pace.

He stopped and turned to face her squarely, his dark eyes dropping to meet hers and locking on them with an intensity that made her immediately uncomfortable.

'What is it?' he asked quietly, calling attention to the shrillness of her voice by the softness of his own.

She compressed het lips into a tight line and looked directly into his eyes, struggling to maintain control. Then suddenly his eyes dropped to her mouth, and she felt her lips part involuntarily under his gaze. He continued to stare at her lips, his eyes moving over them with a slow familiarity that was both insulting and arousing while his own mouth curved sardonically. She felt an almost uncontrollable urge to slap his face, even though her mind told her the reaction was childishly foolish. Taking offence simply because a man looked at her mouth was an insupportable reaction, yet she had never felt so physically violated as she did under his gaze.

'Stop it!' she hissed suddenly, unable to maintain silence.

His dark eyes flickered with knowing amusement.

'Charles!' an enormous voice boomed behind her. A body as massive as the voice it carried moved carefully around her to bang Charles heartily on the shoulder, then a huge, club-like hand attached to the body grabbed Rissom's hand and pumped it furiously. 'Good to see you here! I was afraid I wouldn't have any bidding competition this year!'

Valerie had to tip her head back on her neck to look up at the man's face: a swarthy collection of folds and creases smiling benevolently down on her, topped preposterously by a huge, battered Stetson that cast a circle of shade over the thick stump of his neck.

'And who might this pretty young thing be?' the man asked with a wink.

Charles controlled his distaste for the huge man's brashness with a quick tightening of his jaw that went unnoticed. 'Valerie Smith,' he said formally, 'please meet Harold Perton.'

Valerie gasped as her hand was swallowed in Perton's

bear-like grip, and fought back a cry of alarm as he pumped her hand with only slightly less vigor than he had Rissom's. His obvious delight at meeting her seemed all out of proportion to the circumstances.

'Perton?' she asked hastily, trying to reclaim her hand. 'Of Perton Industries?'

The big man's smile split his face horizontally and his pleased laughter boomed over the background noise around them. 'That's right, little lady. Perton Industries, that's me. Perton Oil, Perton Plastics, Perton Machinery, and of course, Perton Arabians.' His smile spread even further across his open face, and Valerie suddenly liked this enormous bear of a man who obviously took so much pride in his accomplishments.

'Mr Perton,' she smiled sincerely, 'it's a pleasure to meet the man behind the empire.'

She immediately regretted her compliment as his heavy arm wrapped around her shoulders and squeezed until she could barely breathe.

'And it's a pleasure to meet the little woman behind Charles, here,' he confided with a playful jab at Rissom's shoulder.

Valerie frowned, shooting a glance at Rissom, then her face cleared as she realised the conclusion Perton had drawn after hearing her last name.

Charles smiled impassively at the man who loomed a full head taller. 'No, Harold,' he corrected him. 'Valerie and I only happen to share the same last name. No relation at all. In fact, Ms Smith is Jacob's friend.' He drew out the last word with snide implication. 'I'm just keeping her company while Jacob shows Sheikh.'

Perton released her shoulder abruptly and took a step backward, running his eyes up and down her body with a new awareness. 'Oh,' he said awkwardly, 'Jacob's woman, eh?' And then as if that piece of news were enough to discount her completely from any further notice, he wrapped an arm companionably around

Charles' shoulder and turned away from her, speaking only to Charles with his voice lowered to a gravelly whisper.

'Are you bidding this year, Charles? Going to make another million for that Rissom fellow?'

Charles smiled indulgently and pulled politely away, collecting Valerie's arm in the same motion. 'We'll see, Harold. We'll see.'

Perton accepted the obvious dismissal, touched his hat in a jaunty salute, and lumbered off in the opposite direction as he called over his shoulder, 'See you at the auction, Charles!'

Valerie stood ramrod straight as Charles tugged gently at her arm, her face unnaturally flushed, still smarting from the casual dismissal she had sensed when Perton learned she was Jacob's 'woman'.

Charles read her face easily. 'There's an old truism about staying out of the kitchen . . .' he began, but she cut him off with a warning glance of eyes darkened with anger.

'Somehow I don't think you have what it takes to be labelled as "Jacob's Woman",' he said quietly.

'And what would it take?' she asked, snapping out the words.

'Guts,' he answered solemnly. 'And complete indifference to what other people think of you.'

She closed her eyes to the confusion around her and inside her, suddenly tired at the prospect of battling the opinions and judgments of others; especially those of this man. She was desperately homesick for New York, for the quiet assurance she felt moving in her own circles, for the respect always accorded Valerie Kipper. Valerie Smith, whoever she was, was sagging under the weight of deceit.

Charles seemed surprisingly sensitive to her fragile state of mind, and urged her gently over to a large pavilion on one side of the ring, where chairs had been set out in ordered rows under the shade of a massive canopy. He paused briefly before the velvet rope that blocked the entrance to the tent, then unhooked it from the post to which it was attached, and flung it into the dust. The rope lay there like a limp, red velvet snake, small puffs of dust rising from the coils where it had circled over itself.

Valerie pulled herself out of her own silent depression long enough to note the façade of calm across Rissom's face, completely contrary to the fury in the gesture when he had cast the rope aside. He took note of her silent question and answered it.

'I hate discrimination of any kind,' he said coldly. 'And I hate stupidity even more.'

'I don't understand.'

He shook his head in an angry gesture. 'They put this tent up for the stallion owners so they can watch in relative comfort as their horses are presented. But half the seats in here sit empty, while our customers languish out there in the sun. It's just bad business. We should be providing comfort for the people we want to buy our services, not excluding them.'

'Well your opinion should certainly carry some weight. Why haven't you had the policy changed?' she asked reasonably.

His smile was bitter. 'I've learned to live with a lot of things I don't like, just to avoid dealing with people.'

He moved down the long aisle, nodding shortly in response to the enthusiastic greetings he received from some of the other breeders.

'You seem to be remarkably well-received by the same people you have such contempt for,' she pointed out.

'Money is a great friend-maker,' he remarked acidly. 'And a lot of these breeders have something to sell.' He smiled suddenly, a cold, frigid grin that made Valerie shudder. 'They think that I buy horses for Charles

Rissom, and for that reason, most of the people here go out of their way to humour me, although they hate doing it. I have the seat of honour at the Saturday night auction, and everyone stumbles over everyone else trying to make me feel welcome. Money does that. Nothing else.'

The extent of his bitterness amazed her. 'I think you're being unfair. Not all of these people can be like that.'

He stopped in mid-stride and turned to look at her thoughtfully, one brow raised. 'I suppose that's true. I admit I have a tendency to categorise. An experience with one deceitful person can make you forget that there are any honest ones.'

Valerie felt the weight of her own deceit bear down more heavily at his words, but he chuckled suddenly, his eyes distant at some memory that made him smile.

'You know,' he said, 'a few of the breeders here have had the guts to tell me exactly what they think of me, money or not. Those are the ones I respect most, and the ones I deal with, if I can. A lot of them are small breeders, the kind of people that come to affairs like this for one reason: they love their horses. They're special people.' His voice sounded almost wistful, and Valerie felt a pang of sympathy for the man so sadly isolated from his fellow human beings, and wondered again what had made him so bitter.

He moved forward again towards the section reserved for Rissom Farms, dismissing the seriousness of their conversation with a shrug. Valerie was immediately distracted by the people they passed, and her eyebrows lifted in silent acknowledgment of the many familiar faces. She made a mental tally of nineteen she recognised as national newsmakers, and was quietly grateful that she had not interviewed any of them personally.

'I feel like I'm at a meeting of Who's Who in America,' she whispered as they took their seats.

Charles glanced idly around him. 'It's pretty exclusive company, I suppose,' he remarked without interest, then looked at her suddenly, his eyes sparkling with suspicion. 'Is *that* why you hooked up with Jacob? The company he keeps?'

She was taken totally aback, and couldn't think of an appropriate response. He assumed her silence was an admission of sorts, and turned away with an unmistakable expression of disdain.

Valerie tried desperately to stop the laugh as it rolled up her throat and filled her mouth. Valerie Kipper, a celebrity in her own right, being labelled as a namedropper! She and Uncle John would sit around the fire and laugh about this later, and thinking of that made her own laughter uncontrollable, and a small giggle escaped the hand she had pressed to her mouth. Rissom turned to her sharply, and she was sorely tempted to rattle off the names of heads of state and entertainment legends she had interviewed in the last few years, but the ring announcer chose that moment to begin the first stallion's introduction, and her attention to the programme obliterated any thoughts of putting Charles Rissom in his place.

Charles was quietly attentive as the first dozen stallions were brought into the ring, introduced, then led to join their counterparts along the rail. He seemed to straighten slightly in his chair when a particularly animated white stallion floated to his place in centre ring. She detected an uncommon edge of excitement in his voice as he leaned close to her to whisper, 'That's Abdahmen, Sheikh's only real competition this year.'

'Will you buy him?' she asked.

He looked at her in disbelief. 'He's not for sale, and I'm quite sure he never will be. His owner has worked for years to produce an animal of this quality.'

'Then how do you eliminate the competition?'

This time he looked absolutely aghast. 'Eliminate it?

What on earth for? We use it to better our own stock. I have fifteen mares bred to Abdahmen this year, his owner has five of his bred to Sheikh. It's an exciting cross, these two lines. We're both anxious to see what it will produce.'

Valerie looked almost as bewildered as she felt. 'This business is impossible to understand. You compete with each other fiercely, then turn around and use each other's horses.'

He looked at her silently for a long time before he spoke. 'In order to be stimulating,' he said finally, 'competition must be worthy. There's nothing quite as satisfying as finding a competitor equal to the challenge.'

Valerie looked away, uncomfortable. 'Is Abdahmen's owner a friend of yours?'

Charles hesitated for a moment, frowning. 'Not a friend, exactly. We have a business relationship.'

'That seems to be the only kind of relationship you ever have.'

He looked at her sternly. 'It's the only kind worth having. Anyone who thinks otherwise is a fool.'

She began to understand what Jacob meant when he said it was hard to like the man. It wasn't hard; it was impossible. She had never met anyone so totally devoid of human warmth.

'Are your parents alive?' she asked, suddenly curious about what kind of a childhood would harden a man so.

He stared at the activity in the ring for such a long time without answering, that she thought he was ignoring her question. 'No,' he said finally. 'They're both dead.'

The set of his jaw plainly closed that subject to further enquiry, and she wisely remained silent. There would be time enough to ask the questions that needed asking for her article. She didn't want to risk flushing the game too soon.

The loudspeaker crackled slightly as stallion number

fifteen was called to centre ring. A chorus of high-pitched squeals crossed the ring from a group of young girls in the bleachers, and the announcer's amused chuckle echoed through the public address system.

'Ladies and gentlemen,' he announced with a smile that could be heard in his voice. 'If Charles Rissom ever heard the reception his trainer received from the young ladies at horse shows, he might think Jacob Lancer was too much competition for his stallions!'

Laughter rumbled through the crowd, and Valerie looked quickly at Rissom's face to determine his reaction. A small, half-smile played at the corner of his mouth, but his face appeared otherwise calm and indifferent.

'And now,' the announcer proclaimed, 'Jacob Lancer presenting Sheikh el Din of Rissom Farms!'

A burst of wild applause from the bleachers greeted Jacob and Sheikh as they ran into the ring, accompanied by that type of squealing one associates with rock concert audiences. The people around Valerie applauded with the same sedate reserve they had employed for every other stallion presented thus far, and she suspected correctly that they had reason to envy Charles Rissom the attention his trainer commanded.

The crowd's response seemed to electrify the already nervous young stallion, and he appeared as a floating apparition next to Jacob, his head high on the coiled arch of his neck, his hooves snapping to raise tiny whirlwinds of dust. Jacob brought him to a quivering halt at centre ring, guiding him with subtle motions of the short whip to the same posture Valerie had seen earlier at the press conference. When Jacob was finally satisfied with the horse's stance, he and Sheikh immediately went rigid. They were a freeze-frame study of contrasts: Jacob's light hair lifting slightly from his forehead, Sheikh's black mane trailing back over the mighty neck. Horse and man gave each other their full attention, both apparently indifferent to the appreciative murmurs rolling through the audience, and Valerie wasn't certain if the favourable response was directed towards the physical magnificence of the horse, or the man.

'I wonder if they're jealous of each other,' she whispered to Charles, and he responded with a smile rich in amusement.

The announcer read off Sheikh's bloodlines and show record. When he finished, Jacob released the horse from his stand and led him at a high, dancing trot to take his place at the rail. Sheikh challenged the other stallions in the ring with a piercing, high-pitched scream, and reared to paw the air with the fearsome weapons of his front hooves. Valerie caught her breath to see the power of delicate hind legs supporting a body ready for battle, and watched Jacob's quiet, stern mastery as he brought the horse under control. The performance elicited another boisterous response from the young girls in the bleachers, and the announcer jumped at the chance to extract more laughter from his audience.

'Sheikh el Din will be standing at stud at Juniper Farms this year, but I'm sorry to report, young ladies, that Jacob Lancer will not be available to the public. As I understand it, he is accompanied this year by a young woman who has closed his book for the time being.'

Jacob shrugged with a wide, white smile, and there was a rumble of raucous laughter from all sides of the ring. Valerie felt the colour rush up her throat to her face, and leaned over to hiss at Rissom, 'What does he mean, that I've closed his book?'

Rissom laughed out loud, but the laugh was cold and derisive. 'In the horse business,' he explained, 'when you close a stud's book, it means he won't service any other mares.'

Her lips pressed together in a thin line, and the colour fled from her face in a visible retreat, leaving her pale and cold in the afternoon heat. Her legs tensed under her chair, preparing to flee, and she felt rather than saw the contemptuous amusement directed at her from the other people seated in the pavilion. A furious, nauseating knot tightened in her stomach, and her eyes smarted with the sting of unshed tears. Jacob had warned her only yesterday. By tomorrow, he had said, everyone in the Arabian community would know she was his woman, and if the amused glances around her were any indication, he had been right. She remembered Charles telling her it would take guts and indifference to survive being linked with Jacob Lancer, and she grasped at that thought and turned it over in her mind while she struggled for control over emotions that threatened to run away with her. She noted the contempt in Rissom's smile out of the corner of her eye, and was immediately filled with a resolve to hurt this supposedly invincible man. To find his weakness, to exploit it, then plaster it across the pages of the *American Bulletin* for the whole country to see. He who laughs last, she thought grimly, and in that moment, the article on Charles Rissom began to take shape in her mind.

She turned to him quickly, and watched with satisfaction as the pleasure he took in her embarrassment slowly left his face. An ominous determination towards a goal he could not imagine flashed from her eyes in an unspoken challenge, and his own eyes narrowed in a wondering response.

She turned back to face the ring, and sat coolly composed through the remainder of the presentation, never again looking directly at Charles, although he glanced at her often.

After the last stallion had been presented, she rose casually to leave.

'The show classes begin soon,' Rissom reminded her. 'Surely you'll stay to watch Jacob ride.'

'I think not,' she responded with a frigid smile. 'I've been idle too long as it is.'

She walked back to where the velvet rope lay coiled in the dust, and smiled in spite of herself as she stepped over it. Rissom came up quickly behind her and took her elbow gently, almost deferentially.

'Come on. Let's get something cool to drink.'

She remembered the contempt in his smile when she had been embarrassed by the crude words of the announcer, and steeled herself for the job at hand. She would repay his contempt with a vengeance, but she would have to be careful. She mustn't appear too eager.

'Are you sure being seen with me is wise?' she asked with light sarcasm. 'It would seem I'm a marked woman.'

He frowned, then pulled her less gently to walk beside him. 'Sarcasm never becomes a woman,' he remarked coldly.

Her laughter was mirthless. 'Apparently I have many unbecoming qualities. So what is it that attracts you? Why do you want to spend time with me anyway?' Although she began the question only to keep the conversation alive, to force Rissom to reveal qualities in himself that would provide meat for her article, she realised with a slight pang that she was anxiously awaiting his answer for more personal reasons.

'I'm not sure,' he mused as they continued to walk. 'Curiosity, of course, or perhaps you'd prefer to believe that I'm irresistibly drawn to you for purely physical reasons. That would please you, wouldn't it?'

She stopped suddenly and stared directly into his eyes, and the words escaped her lips before she could stop them. 'You are.' She blushed then, and looked down quickly. She hadn't intended to say that.

'Of course I am,' he admitted easily as he moved forward again, pulling her along with him. 'But it doesn't mean anything. It's happened before. I'll take you once, and the desire will be gone.'

'Really,' she answered with equal calm, although a trembling fury consumed her. 'And what makes you think I'd be a consenting partner?'

He stopped walking and turned to face her. 'You were last night,' he said matter-of-factly, 'and you will be again.'

She took a deep breath to keep from screaming, and coloured with shame as she remembered her willingness the night before. 'I had too much to drink last night,' she said quietly, forcing herself to look him in the eye as she lied.

He merely smiled and shook his head. 'Nonsense.'

'It will never happen again,' she said more firmly.

'We'll see,' he replied, and the promise and the threat in those two words hung uncomfortably between them as they walked.

He led her behind the stallion barn and down a narrow asphalt walkway. It meandered through a brief stand of thick brush before opening onto a large, tree-studded parking area.

'Where are we going?' she asked, her eyes taking in the elegant caravans parked like quiet sentinels across the grassy lot.

'I promised you a cool drink, remember?' he answered, and guided her to an end space where a sleek white caravan stood in relative isolation.

'This is yours? You drove here?'

'It's mine, but I didn't drive here. I had one of the grooms bring it down from the farm.'

'Why? Surely it would have been much more practical to stay in a hotel.'

'I'm not a practical man, Ms Smith. And I hate hotels,' he said shortly.

He unlocked the vehicle's side door and motioned her up the three steps with a wave of his hand. She entered the blessedly cool, air-conditioned interior and breathed a heavy sigh of relief.

'Have a seat,' he invited as he followed her in and closed the door on the heat behind him.

She slid into the plush upholstered bench that enclosed a round table of burnished wood in a cozy half-circle. Her eyes flickered at her surroundings with interest while he busied himself at the refrigerator.

'This doesn't look much like the caravans I've seen,' she remarked, noting the deep pile of the plush carpeting and the gleam of hand-rubbed wood. 'There's no plastic.'

His chuckle was punctuated with the musical sound of ice cubes tinkling against crystal. 'The interior was a custom job. Plastic offends me, and all of the line models were nothing but. Here you are.'

She noted the weight of the cut crystal glass in an automatic appreciation of all beautiful things, and delighted at the cooling vision of a bright lime slice bobbing in the clear liquid. 'Thank you,' she murmured, taking a tentative sip. He slid into the bench seat opposite her, draining half of his own glass before setting it down.

She felt his eyes on her as she continued to take in the caravan's polished, quiet elegance, and was as disturbed by his frank examination as she was by the environment. Suddenly she realised what bothered her about the vehicle, and turned to face him with a question that died on her lips when her eyes met his.

He looked up from lowered brows that cast an ominous shadow across the sharp angles of his face, and his graciousness of a moment before was lost in an expression of cruel intolerance. In that single moment, Valerie felt brutal power emanating from the man, and realised how formidable a foe he would become when he discovered her deception. Her hands twisted together under the table and she remained speechless under his gaze. His eyes cleared suddenly, then closed as he tipped up his glass and drained the contents.

'You were going to ask me something,' he said casually as he moved to refill his glass.

She nodded mutely, then caught herself wavering under the spell of his awesome, silent control, and snapped back to attention. 'Yes. About this.' She gestured with her hand to indicate the caravan. 'Is it new?'

'No. It's two years old. Why? Is it starting to look the worse for wear?' He spoke conversationally, as if there had been no long, quiet moment quivering with menace, and his very casualness was disconcerting.

'On the contrary,' she answered. 'It looks like it just came off the production line.'

He freshened her drink without asking, then rejoined her at the table. An errant lock of glossy black slipped down over his forehead, softening his face. 'Actually, this machine has taken me back and forth across the country several times. I'll have to replace it soon.'

'That's extraordinary,' she said, looking around her. 'It looks almost unused. Like a model home. A place where people have never lived.'

He smiled grimly. 'I've heard that before. About this, about my penthouse in New York, and a few other places I've lived. One rather disturbed young woman told me once I left no trace of myself anywhere. That when I was gone, it was as if I never existed at all.' His lips twisted into an unpleasant smile. 'In fact, I believe she told me that that would be my epitaph: "Charles Rissom. He left nothing behind."'

Valerie frowned as she watched lines of bitterness pull at his face, wondering what the young woman had been like, and if he had treated her badly. For the moment, her sympathy was automatically with the girl.

'And what did she say about your farm in Minnesota?' she asked with a lightness she didn't feel.

His eyes narrowed to focus intensely on hers. 'She said

nothing. She never saw it. No one has.'

'Jacob has,' she countered.

'That was necessary. Business demanded that Jacob spend time there, otherwise he never would have. The farm is private,' he concluded harshly.

His face closed to her, like the clang of an iron door, and she found herself wondering what it must be like to live in a home where no one was welcomed, without family, without friends, without the simple warmth of human companionship she took so much for granted. She voiced her musings aloud without thinking. 'No one but Jacob has ever seen your farm?'

'No one.'

'Not even . . .' She shrugged, unable to phrase the question delicately, and he laughed at her reticence.

'No. Not even the women I have known. Not one.'

She tipped her head and stared at him thoughtfully, no longer trying to mask her curiosity. 'It must be lonely there,' she said softly, preparing herself for a vehement denial.

Instead, he merely acknowledged the statement with a toasting gesture of his glass. 'It can be,' he admitted freely. 'But then sometimes we compromise, sacrifice one thing in order to achieve another.'

'And what have you achieved by sacrificing the companionship of other human beings? What could possibly be worth that?'

'Something I value above all things. Privacy.'

'You've paid a high price for it.'

He shrugged. 'It's worth it.'

He shifted suddenly in his seat and stared at her thoughtfully. 'What do you see in Jacob, anyway?' he asked suddenly.

She frowned at the implication that Jacob had little to offer. 'You don't think much of him, do you?' she accused.

'On the contrary. I think a great deal of Jacob. So

much so, in fact, that his infatuation with you worries me.'

She bristled automatically. 'For a man who values privacy so highly, you have the most disconcerting habit of intruding into other people's affairs.'

He raised one eyebrow and smiled coldly. 'I'm fond of Jacob. Warning him about you is on a plane with warning him if he were about to be run over by a truck. I don't consider either warning a violation of his privacy.'

She jumped to her feet and leaned across the table to hiss into his face. 'What is it that makes you so much better than the rest of us, Mr Rissom? How can you possibly judge and condemn others so quickly?'

He looked up at her calmly. 'Relax, Ms Smith. I haven't finished judging you, yet. If I had, Jacob would have known this morning that you were mine last night—or would have been, if I'd chosen to take you.'

The air built up inside her lungs until they felt like they would explode. She released the pressure with a sharp exhale that left her dizzy, and slightly sick to her stomach. 'You don't understand what happened last night,' she said lamely, slumping back into her seat.

'You're right,' he answered with an edge to his voice. 'But I'm willing to listen. How do you explain your eagerness to hop from bed to bed, and man to man? I can hardly wait to hear it.'

She caught her lower lip between her teeth, and fought once more the impulse to tell him the truth. 'What would you say, Mr Rissom,' she began softly, 'if I told you that what happened between us last night had nothing whatever to do with my relationship to Jacob?'

'I would say that you're probably the coldest, most amoral woman I've ever met,' he answered quickly.

She blinked at him slowly, abandoning any thoughts of confessing to the harsh, censorious man before her that she had been foolish enough to mistake him for

Prince Charming. 'Forget it,' she said sadly, shaking her head.

'I'm not about to forget last night, Ms Smith,' he said steadily. 'And I don't think you will, either.'

The accuracy of his last statement hit the mark, but her reaction was not what he had expected. She was suddenly tired of his arrogant self-righteousness, and even more tired of being on the defensive. 'Well, I'm going to give it a try,' she said dully. 'Thanks for the drink.'

He stopped her with his hand as she moved to rise from the table. 'You're in fast company, Ms Smith. I'd think long and hard, if I were you, before using people. You may regret it.'

She pulled her arm away from his grasp with an angry jerk. 'You'd know all about using people, wouldn't you?' she demanded furiously. 'You're an expert!'

He dropped his chin to his chest in a submissive gesture, but raised his eyes to look at her, and the posture reminded her oddly of a little boy contemplating mischief. The notion was dispelled by his reply.

'Yes, I'm an expert. I've been used by the best of them. America's press.'

He could barely contain a smile when she reached quickly for her glass, and nearly choked on the first swallow. 'What do you mean?' she asked hoarsely.

He ran one dark hand back through the black tangle of his hair, and Valerie found the gesture strangely appealing. 'Let's just say I had a . . . difficult childhood.'

Her eyes sparkled with interest, but her voice was controlled. 'Oh?'

He tipped his head and stared at her thoughtfully for a long moment, as if he were measuring her, then his face grew hard with determination. 'I learned the value of privacy from my father,' he said finally, 'and have guarded mine jealously ever since. The users can't reach you if they don't know who you are.'

Her mind switched on like a tape recorder, and she had to tighten her hands into fists to keep them from scrambling in her purse for a notebook and pen. This was the background she had been waiting for. 'Your father?' she asked with what she hoped would sound like idle curiosity. 'Who was your father?'

There was an instant when she thought she detected amusement in his eyes, but it passed quickly, and his face was solemn. 'Martin Vasslar,' he said quietly, and she responded with a low, breathy whistle. 'I'm surprised you know the name,' he said. 'It was well before your time.'

'It's history,' she replied, still wide-eyed with amazement. 'You're Martin Vasslar's *son*?'

'A rose by any other name . . .' he said sarcastically. 'Rissom was one of my grandmother's maiden names. After my father died, it seemed wise to bury the entire family, figuratively, of course. Do you know the story?'

She hesitated, unsure of what his reaction would be when such things were put into words, but if anything, his smile seemed encouraging. 'He was a special adviser to the President,' she began tentatively. 'Accused of espionage, tried, and found guilty. He committed suicide before he was sentenced, and his wife and only son simply disappeared.'

He nodded slowly. 'Very good. High school history served you well. What the course may not have mentioned was that he slashed his wrists in his own bathroom while members of the noble press banged on the front door.' He sighed deeply, then continued in a perfunctory manner, as if he were reciting a lesson from memory. 'I was nine at the time, and foolish enough to open the door. The reporters found my father's body at the same time my mother did, and I have a vague memory of flashbulbs popping as my mother screamed. It was difficult to sustain any admiration for the press after that, or for the public. They were like vultures, feeding on other people's pain, heedless of the lives they violated, sacrificing anything for the questionable virtue of getting the story.'

'It must have been horrible,' she whispered, 'but not all people are like that. Not anymore.'

His smile was grim. 'Aren't they?'

A melting ice cube clinked against the side of her glass with an inappropriately merry sound. 'What did your mother do then?' she asked softly, and her voice sounded distant, as if someone else had spoken. 'Where did you go?'

'We hopped from town to town for a long time. She waited on tables, mostly. Imagine that,' he said softly, his eyes focused on some distant point in the past. 'A woman who dined with Presidents as a waitress in a truckstop. She died when I was fourteen,' he finished flatly.

'And you?'

'Me?' His laugh was cold and bitter. 'I became rich and famous, and hid from the press.'

In a totally unexpected gesture, he reached across the table and captured her hand in his. 'Well, Ms Smith,' he said, turning her hand upside down and examining the lines in her palm. 'There you have the reason for my obsessive code of privacy. Does it please you to be privy to such secrets?'

She let her hand rest quietly under his inspection, oddly content to be sitting in silence, as long as he was touching her. 'What you told me,' she said finally. 'It must be the best-kept secret in the world.'

He looked up slowly, and his smile was almost bemused. 'It should be. Until a few moments ago, I was the only person alive who knew the story.'

Valerie's forehead wrinkled in an amazed frown. 'Then why . . . ?'

'. . . did I tell you?' His smile broadened. 'Business,

Ms Smith. Every decision I make is based on one thing—whether or not it's good for business.'

'That doesn't make sense. I don't understand. How could telling me all this possibly be good for business?'

'I don't expect you to understand. Not now. But someday you will. Believe me.'

She watched blankly as he rose from the table, wearing one of the few genuine smiles she had seen on his face. It softened the angles into strong, flowing curves, and made him infinitely attractive.

'I imagine you'd like to return to your hotel before dinner,' he said. 'Then perhaps you'd allow me to take you somewhere a little out of the ordinary.'

'I'm sorry,' she answered with genuine regret, 'but I can't. I promised Jacob I'd meet him at six-thirty in the motel restaurant. I should hurry, or I'll never have time to change,' she added as she glanced at her watch.

'Another time then,' he said easily, and she felt a pang of dismay that he wasn't more visibly disappointed. 'If I may make a suggestion, I'd recommend formal attire if you're dining at the motel this evening. The owners of the horses that will be sold at auction Saturday meet at your motel tonight, and the occasion is traditionally white tie.'

'Jacob never mentioned it,' she said lamely, and Charles laughed.

'He wouldn't think of it. It has absolutely nothing to do with a horse.'

'Will you be there?'

'As a buyer of one of last year's auction horses Rissom Farms was invited, yes.' He raised his brows with a speculative smile. 'And I think I may go after all.'

He watched through the window as she walked away, satisfied that he had done what was necessary to protect himself, and bitter that it had been necessary at all. It rankled to have been forced into a lie, and such a preposterous one at that. Martin Vasslar, indeed!

CHAPTER NINE

VALERIE eyed herself critically in the full-length mirror in her room. She was totally uncomfortable at the prospect of walking down the motel corridor past children in swimsuits and adults in casual attire, dressed in a gown she had worn last at a Mideastern coronation. Perhaps it was a trick, she thought. Charles Rissom's idea of a colossal joke, seeing her dressed to the hilt in a room full of blue jeans and straw hats. She shook her head at her reflection, discounting the notion. Rissom was above that sort of backyard humour; of that, she was certain.

She had barely had time to shower, wash her hair and change as it was, and every moment was doubly consumed with reviewing Rissom's startling disclosure over and over again in her mind. She didn't want to forget a word of it, and she wouldn't have time to make notes until she returned to her room much later. If she made notes at all, that is.

He had confided in her for a reason she couldn't begin to understand, but with that confidence came responsibility, and it weighed heavily on her.

Time and again in her career she had been told secrets 'off the record', and honouring that request was part of what made her such an excellent journalist. She had never betrayed a source, or printed material she felt would harm the subject irreparably, and she faced that choice now. The man baffled her completely. He was hostile one moment, and gracious the next, and she wasn't yet certain which was the real man, and which the façade. On the two occasions when they had been truly alone together, there had been a warm, easy cama-

78

raderie that couldn't be faked. His attraction to her had to be every bit as real as her attraction to him. And yet the contempt that he demonstrated at other times, the disdain that shattered the promise of those private times, was every bit as real, and so powerful that it completely negated any tenderness he displayed. Surely his knowledge of the relationship she supposedly shared with Jacob wasn't enough to justify the extent of his cruelty, but what other reason could there be? She felt as though she was on a madman's teeter totter: high with hope for a split second in time, only to be plummeted to the depths of despair. Her vacillation between whether to write the article or not had to stop soon. A decision would have to be made. She sighed deeply, knowing the decision was out of her hands. Charles Rissom would make it himself.

The gown was a floor-length sheath of sable brown that dropped elegantly across her breasts from one shoulder, leaving the other totally bare. Gold metallic threads were woven into the fabric so cleverly that at first glance, one could not see the threads themselves; only the dazzling effect they produced. The skirt was slit on one side to above the knee, showing much less leg than she had displayed earlier in her walking shorts, but the result was erotically sensuous with the rest of her body so modestly covered. Her hair fell in full, natural waves across her shoulders, and the golden highlights in the rich, toasty brown vied for attention with the subtle shimmer of her dress. She declined jewellery, the dress itself being ornament enough, and nodded briefly to her reflection before leaving the room.

The dining room had been cordoned off to regular guests for the evening, and a discreet wooden easel bore an elaborate parchment scroll welcoming the patrons of the Egyptian Arabian horse.

She heard the plaintive strains of violins in the background as she approached the entrance, and then she saw Jacob. He was immersed in an animated conversation with a man whose back was to Valerie, and the sweep of Jacob's white-blond hair quivered with the intensity of his remarks. He caught sight of her over the shorter man's shoulder, then paid her one of the most extraordinary compliments she had ever received.

He stopped talking in mid-sentence, and with his lips frozen open in the position that had formed his last word, he extended one arm thoughtlessly and pushed his companion to one side, out of the range of his vision. The man turned in obvious indignation to see the object of Jacob's attention and the cause for his inexplicable rudeness, and his angry face softened into a semblance of understanding appreciation when he saw Valerie.

Her lips curved into a smile of greeting for Jacob, and it was with a quiet voice of thanks to Charles Rissom that she noted his white tie and tails.

Jacob's eyes darkened almost imperceptibly as they travelled the full length of her body in an appraisal that was remarkably intimate without being rude. She felt a vague, pleasant tingle at the nape of her neck as his eyes rested on hers when she finally stopped in front of him, and his silence was eloquent.

'Hello, Jacob,' she said softly, and he made no response save for the tightening of muscles that held his jaw strongly set, and the slight lowering of his eyelids.

Without taking his eyes from hers, and in full view of anyone who cared to look, he reached out with the fingers of one hand and traced a tantalising line up from her wrist to her bare shoulder, lingering there for a brief moment before threading through the thickness of her hair to rest quietly around her neck. She tipped her head to one side until her cheek touched his hand, and felt his fingers tighten convulsively as he lowered his head to touch her lips lightly with his. He pulled back quickly, his eyes narrowed and vibrantly deep, then straightened with a quivering exhale, as if he had already revealed too much.

Valerie marvelled at the gentle warmth spreading through her body in response to the touch of a man she had thought of only as a friend, and returned his gaze with a new awareness.

Then Jacob glanced around furtively, like a young boy who suspects his mischievous pranks might have been observed, and shattered the spell like a hammer cracking a mirror.

'Oh, Jacob!' she murmured in disappointment, but he took her feeble exclamation as an expression of passion, and grinned with schoolboy pride, as if he had just made the winning touchdown.

She shook her head in amused resignation as Jacob led her into the dining room, but a deep sorrow for what might have been twisted her quiet smile downward slightly. The diners who turned in their chairs to watch the entrance of the golden couple could not read her expression, with the single exception of Charles Rissom. He sat at the head of the table reserved for Rissom Farms, his face dark and ominous, his eyes riveted on Valerie's face. No one noticed his earnest concentration.

Jacob's proud, puffed stride was nearly a strut as he guided Valerie to the Rissom table, standing a little apart from her as if to better show her to the crowd. She had the uncomfortable feeling of being presented, as if she were one of his horses. The feeling intensified when her glance happened upon Rissom's sardonic smile as he rose at her approach, and her throat constricted in sudden disappointment. The afternoon's intimacy was gone without a trace, just as she had feared it would be, and his face registered nothing but contemptuous amusement.

She sat quickly at his right, with Jacob on her right,

and met Charles' eyes fully. 'Enjoying yourself, Mr Smith?'

'I'm about to,' he answered mysteriously.

The first part of the evening passed painfully for Valerie as she felt the eyes of others in the room return to her again and again. There seemed to be a constant undercurrent of whispers, and she imagined that many of them concerned her.

One woman in particular, seated at the table adjacent to theirs, punctuated her continuous buzzing with malevolent glances directed towards Valerie. At one point midway through the dinner she announced in a voice plainly meant to be heard, 'Well, the supply is obviously endless. I've never seen him with the same one twice. But I, personally, could never allow myself to be so *used*.'

Valerie coloured visibly, and Jacob leaned over the back of his chair to address the woman directly. 'Mrs Harrington,' he said with a dazzling smile that made her titter and flutter like a matronly bird, 'I can almost guarantee that there is absolutely no danger of that ever happening.'

The woman gasped in red-faced affront, Valerie suppressed a smile, and Charles' laughter filled the room.

'Very, very good, Jacob,' he congratulated him with good humour. 'I couldn't have done better myself.'

'I'm sorry, Valerie,' Jacob mumbled under his breath. 'I should never have exposed you to this. It's entirely my fault.'

She smiled with genuine fondness at his crestfallen face, and touched his cheek lightly with her hand.

'It's all right, Jacob,' she reassured him. 'That woman only put into words what everyone has been thinking anyway. It doesn't make it harder just to hear it finally said aloud. Besides, I knew what I was getting into from the beginning, and I decided then that it was worth it.'

Charles listened to the exchange with glowering

interest, and when he finally spoke, his voice was cold. 'This is all very touching,' he said sarcastically, and Valerie turned towards him slowly, recognising the cruel contempt in his tone. Her eyes flickered briefly over his in a dismayed realisation of the situation in which she found herself. Her statement to Jacob, intended only as words of comfort, had apparently convinced the one man whose opinion mattered that her relationship with the flamboyant trainer was real, and permanent.

Charles glanced at Jacob, and for a moment, his grim smile was almost sympathetic. Then he turned to Valerie with an expression she would remember later as frightening, and spoke quietly. 'I think Ms Smith deserves better, Jacob, don't you? A public exoneration perhaps?'

Jacob frowned slightly, acutely aware of Charles' hostility towards Valerie, but uncertain as to its cause. 'What do you mean?' he asked suspiciously.

'It's very simple,' Charles replied evenly. 'If you really care for this woman, I think you should save her further embarrassment by declaring your intentions. Make an honest woman of her, so to speak.'

Jacob recognised the challenge, and the slur against Valerie, and jumped to her defence, his face flushed with indignant sincerity. 'I'd marry Valerie in a minute!' he proclaimed.

Rissom nodded with an unpleasant smile. 'I thought so,' he said, and rose dramatically to his feet, his eyes boring into Valerie's as if to emphasise that he knew precisely what he was doing, and found it infinitely pleasurable.

'Ladies and gentlemen,' he announced in rounded tones that carried throughout the room, even though he hadn't raised his voice. He tapped his spoon lightly against the side of his water goblet, and all eyes turned immediately towards him as the room hushed. 'It would seem we are all unwitting parties to a celebration of sorts. Jacob Lancer has just announced his intention to take Ms Valerie Smith as his wife.'

There was a thunderous round of applause that neither Jacob nor Valerie heard. His face was open in amazed disbelief, hers was a sheet of white with only two hot spots of red indicating where colour had been just a moment before.

Rissom had left no denial possible for either of them, and Jacob squirmed in his seat as he reached for Valerie's hand and pressed it into a palm suddenly cold and clammy. 'My God, Valerie! I don't know what he's doing!' he whispered under the clamour of voices that followed.

Valerie squeezed his hand lightly, then withdrew her own, unconsciously drying it on the napkin in her lap. 'Neither does he, Jacob,' she said stonily. 'Neither does he.'

'What are we going to do?'

'We're going to smile, Jacob. Like a good, happy couple. Just smile.'

There was a flurry of hand-shaking and back-clapping as everyone in the room pressed around the table to wish the couple well. Valerie remained elegantly poised as she pressed a dozen hands and murmured polite thank-yous, while Rissom watched her face intently with eyes violently dark and a frozen smile.

Jacob began accepting hearty, sometimes ribald congratulations with the wariness of a confused puppy, but quickly warmed to the attention. He became so caught up in the pretended role of blustering bridegroom-to-be, that he began to believe the charade they were creating, or at least to believe in its possibility. When the confusion died, he sat happily next to Valerie, flushed with excitement, thinking that marriage might not be such a bad idea after all, even if the idea hadn't been his. The quiet menace in Valerie's voice shattered the illusion quickly.

'You enjoy manipulating people, don't you, Mr Smith?' she asked Charles quietly. Her face was a mask of composure, her voice entirely controlled, and oddly disturbing. 'I will remember this night for a very long time, thanks to you,' she continued. 'But you will remember it, too. I promise you that.'

And then she excused herself suddenly, pleading exhaustion to Jacob, insisting that he remain.

Valerie maintained her exterior calm until she reached her room, but once the door slammed shut behind her, she flung her evening bag against the wall, breaking the clasp and sending the contents flying. She stormed to the bedside phone and stabbed viciously at the buttons until John's telephone in New York rang on the other end of the line. Telling him about the article she intended to write would solidify her commitment, and at the moment, that gesture would give her immense satisfaction. The telephone rang three times, then there was an abrupt click as the answering machine turned on. She slammed down the receiver in the middle of the recorded message, refusing to share her news with a machine, and began to pace in frustration.

She stopped suddenly and snatched a blank legal pad from the top of the writing desk, and scrawled across the top sheet in bold, slashing strokes: 'Charles Rissom: The Truth About America's Man of Mystery'.

She straightened and looked at the words she had written, and though she still quivered with rage, she could not yet bring herself to put in black and white the story that would destroy the man. She flung the pen on the desk in disgust at her own weakness, and resumed pacing until the room seemed like a cage of walls slowly closing in on her. On impulse she shovelled the scattered contents of her evening bag into a larger bag, snatched her car keys from the dresser, and stormed from the room.

She drove aimlessly through downtown Lexington,

the car windows open wide, the radio blasting. She lost her way twice, and finally had to stop at a petrol station for directions back to her motel.

Once back on the freeway, the heavy night air buffetting her face and throwing her hair into tangles she would regret later, she began to calm down. She switched off the radio's meaningless sounds with a twist of her hand. The speed itself was both intoxicating and soothing, and she breathed in deep, cleansing breaths of the warm, humid air. She sped past the exit to her motel unintentionally, but only shrugged. She was still too restless for the confines of her room.

Within a few moments she found herself at the entrance to the Kentucky Horse Park, and turned automatically into the long, curving drive. It seemed perfectly natural that she should have ended up there. It was the only place in Lexington she knew.

She instinctively took the left fork in the road that led to the breeders' parking lot, and stopped the car next to Rissom's caravan as if she had every right to be there. She hesitated before leaving her car, then assured herself that Rissom would be at the breeders' dinner for hours, and would never know of her presence in the deserted park.

The subdued glow of lights from the stallion barn drew her like a magnet, and she made her way up the asphalt walkway, holding her skirt high above evening sandals. The barn was apparently deserted, and once inside the door she heard the contented munching of horses finishing hay, the occasional rustle of hooves moving over heavy bedding, and the odd, sleepy nickering of one communicative stallion. She sank quietly on to a bench by the door and leaned back against the wall with her eyes closed. The gentle night noises of the barn were strangely soothing, and for the first time in many hours, she felt at peace with herself.

She had been resting there only a few moments when

her mind discerned a sound that had no place in the deserted barn: the sound of a human voice. She straightened in alarm, her eyes wide in the dim lighting, and tried to locate the source of the voice. She finally pinpointed it at the Rissom stalls. A groom, probably, soothing an anxious horse; performing whatever functions one performed to settle a horse for the night.

She was slightly uncomfortable at the prospect of being discovered in the barn at all, especially dressed as she was. How would she explain her presence there to a stranger? Then she remembered with a rueful smile that she had just been publicly declared Jacob Lancer's betrothed, and where he had a right to be, she had a right to be.

She slipped noiselessly down the aisle next to the stalls, her slender heels sinking deeply into the sawdust. Although her curiosity was aroused, she would be happily content to discover who else was in the barn, then steal silently away without being discovered herself.

As she moved closer to the stall that housed the prized Sheikh el Din, she saw the shadow loom across the centre aisle that indicated a human presence in with the horse, and she held her breath to better hear the words the low voice was speaking. Murmured softly, they were blurred and indistinct, and she crept closer still to stand in front of the adjacent stall before she recognised the voice as Charles Rissom's.

Surprise, and then remembered anger flashed across her face. She had half-turned to leave when the words she overheard stopped her.

'I'm sorry, boy,' Rissom was whispering. 'I'm really sorry.'

Valerie pressed herself tightly against the wall and inched forward step by silent step, drawn by the anguish in Rissom's voice.

'It's been a long time, fellah, I know,' the words

continued. 'And you don't understand, do you? You don't know why you're here. You only want to go home . . .'

The voice cracked, and had it been less sincere, less pained, Valerie would have found this obvious apology to an animal laughable. As it was, her eyes clouded in confusion. This was a side of Charles Rissom she had never seen. She guessed that few people had.

The horse nickered an encouraging response, and Rissom began speaking again. His voice lowered to a hoarse whisper, and Valerie took another step forward and moved her head slightly to peek through the open bars of the stall door.

The man and the horse were both facing away from her, Rissom's left arm flung across Sheikh's mighty neck, his right hand moving in gentle, stroking motions from the forelock down to the soft muzzle. Valerie didn't know which was more remarkable: seeing Rissom in such an open emotional display, or seeing the frightening stallion so totally subdued.

The horse's tightly muscled neck was extended forward and down, his head stretched towards Rissom's hand to better receive the stroking caress. The large, dark eyes were closed, the nostrils quivering with the force of deep, relaxed breaths. Whenever the soothing sounds of his master's voice ceased, Sheikh responded with a nicker, and Valerie shook her head in wonder to witness such an exchange. It was as close to conversation as could be possible between man and animal.

Rissom's head dropped suddenly to rest on Sheikh's neck, and for a moment the gloss of the black mane and Rissom's equally dark hair mingled, and she could not distinguish between them.

'We're a pair, you know,' Rissom whispered. 'Both of us doing a job we don't particularly like, both of us wishing we were home.'

The horse nickered a response.

'But you've got it better than I have, boy. Believe me. When the season's over, you'll go home, and there's a lot more waiting for you than there is for me.'

The stallion butted Rissom's hand, prodding for more vigorous attention. Charles complied by scratching behind the short, pricked ears, and the horse exhaled with pleasure.

Rissom turned to pat the horse's flank affectionately, his hand jerking to a halt in mid-air when he saw Valerie peering through the bars.

His face reflected total surprise, then hostility. 'What the hell are you doing here?' he demanded, and Sheikh responded to the sudden anger in his master's voice by whirling quickly in the stall until he, too, faced Valerie. His eyes rolled back at the unexpected materialisation of an unfamiliar human, and his nostrils flared with the heavy blows that were both an attempt to identify the strange presence, and a threatened challenge if it should prove unfriendly.

Valerie jerked away from the door in fright at the animal's sudden movements and wild appearance, and the very quickness of her own retreat triggered an age-old apprehension in the stallion. He immediately reared back on his hind legs and pawed the air with his front hooves, and even though the heavy stall door was between them, Valerie gave a small cry of alarm and stumbled backward, falling ingloriously into the sawdust. She scrambled quickly to her feet in the same instinctive response of her counterparts in the horse family, and prepared to flee.

Rissom's low chuckle reflected the comic picture she must have presented, and she swallowed her indignation, grateful that he had temporarily forgotten his anger at her intrusion. He peered at her through the bars of the stall door and smiled crookedly. 'Never let a horse intimidate you,' he warned gently. 'Especially not this one.'

'I'd say that warning could apply equally well to dealing with you,' she muttered hotly, attempting to brush off the back of her dress while still retaining some dignity.

Sheikh moved up next to Rissom to press his muzzle against the bars, and Valerie prudently backed away.

'That horse is a killer,' she pronounced with conviction, and Charles answered with a short laugh as Sheikh reached up to nose his ear. He stroked the stallion's neck absently, pressing his ear against his shoulder to escape the tickling muzzle.

'This horse is a baby,' he answered, 'as even you should be able to see.'

She brushed the dust from her hands in a businesslike fashion and eyed the horse from under lowered brows, as if he were a mortal enemy. 'To you he's a baby; to me, he's a killer.'

'Valerie.'

He pronounced her name with a wistfulness that caught at her heart and twisted, and she raised her eyes to meet his.

'I want you to come in here with me.'

She stared at him as if he had just asked her to jump off the Empire State Building, and merely shook her head in disbelief that he could even suggest such a thing.

'Please.'

She found her voice and her legs at the same time, and began backing away warily. 'Please?' she echoed. 'You want me "please" to come in there and be eaten, or trampled, or whatever it is that horses do to people?' Her eyes and her mouth made perfect, amazed circles, and Charles laughed as he slid open the stall door. She scrambled even further back, and felt the race of her own heart.

'Valerie. Don't run. Wait,' he said gently.

She noticed with some embarrassment that he was

using the same soothing tone on her he had used earlier
with the horse.

'How long were you standing outside this stall?' he
asked suddenly, and a stern note crept into his voice.

She felt the same guilt she would have felt had she
eavesdropped on a sinner's confession, and looked
down at the floor meekly. She knew instinctively that the
depth of Rissom's pride would be cut deeply by her
observance of emotions he assumed others would think
a sign of weakness, and tried to lie to spare him.

'Not very long,' she whispered.

His smile was grim, but knowing, and he shook his
head. 'Sorry. I don't buy that. I'd guess you were there
long enough to paint me as a fool.'

'I didn't think it was foolish,' she put in quickly.

'A conversation with a horse? Come on. Of course
you did. And you'll continue to think so, unless I make
you understand. You eavesdropped, and you were
caught. You owe me something for that.'

She worried her lower lip with her teeth as she
frowned, nervously shifting her weight from one foot to
the other. 'It was an accident,' she began. 'I didn't mean
to . . .'

'Nevertheless, you did. You caught me at a weak
moment, and I don't like to be caught at weak moments.
All I'm asking in exchange is that you meet this horse. It
isn't so much, is it?'

'It's everything,' she whispered fearfully. 'I'm
terrified!'

Charles held his hand out through the stall door, his
other continuing to stroke Sheikh's neck as the dainty
head drooped sleepily. 'Look at it this way. First of all,
it's high time you conquered this unreasonable fear of
yours, and I'm going to help you do it. Secondly . . .' He
paused uncertainly and his brow quivered as he searched
for the right words. 'Secondly, it's important to me. I'm
asking a favour.'

His voice had lowered to a whisper Valerie had to strain to hear, and the last words were forced out at a cost she could see in his eyes. She wondered if he had ever asked anyone for a favour before.

She took a deep breath and closed her eyes briefly, then put her shoulders back and moved forward with the stiff-legged gait of someone walking bravely to their death.

She was inches away from the stall door, her eyes wide with terror, when her courage deserted her abruptly and she began to back quietly away. His hand flashed to grab hers, and she pulled against it and whispered, 'I'm sorry! I can't! Please let me go! He'll know I'm afraid. He'll attack me. I know he will!'

As if to confirm her words. Sheikh wakened from his doze with an upward jerk of his head, and eyed her suspiciously through the open space where bars had once separated them. Valerie trembled helplessly while Charles pulled gently on her hand, reeling her in with steady, unyielding persistence. She was forced to take a mincing step forward to avoid falling on her face, and that step put her captive hand within reach of Sheikh's curious, quivering muzzle. Charles abruptly turned his hand over to put Valerie's on top, and the stallion's nose promptly came in contact with her upturned palm. Valerie stiffened instantly.

Fully prepared to see her hand disappear into the horse's powerful jaws, she remained rigid as the velvet muzzle nudged her stiffened fingers, her mouth open and ready to scream, her heart thudding in her chest.

Sheikh smelled the fear of the strange human, and though he watched her carefully for signs of imminent threat, the smell of his master mingling with the smell of this new hand tempered his own timidity, and he continued his snorting investigation. There was no warning as his great tongue descended to her palm, and the hairs on the back of Valerie's neck raised and quivered in response to the steady licking. The sensation was extraordinary, and she could not suppress the nervous giggle, nor the reflex that curled her hand when the giant tongue crossed her palm, and suddenly her fingers touched the velvet softness between the flaring nostrils, and a tiny smile of wonder touched her face.

She took a step forward in daring, moving her hand up the muzzle tentatively, sensing the stubble of recently shaved hairs under her fingertips. She moved only her eyes to look questioningly at Charles, and he smiled at the childlike delight in her face. 'You shave horses?' she asked, and he nodded.

Sheikh moved his head up and down under her hand to encourage patting, and she complied unconsciously, running her fingers up the side of his head, pausing to feel the delicate pulsing of prominent veins, the flat smoothness of the full jowl, the hard, boney proturbances above the eyes. Her smile widened as her fingers delighted with the sensations they were transmitting rapidly to her brain. Charles smiled broadly as she walked into the stall, knowing she was not aware that she had done so.

When Valerie's hands finally moved to Sheikh's ears, he groaned with deep-throated pleasure and tipped his head first to one side, then the other, finally thrusting his muzzle directly into her midriff in an expression of ultimate trust. The hot breath from the nostrils pressed against her permeated the thin fabric of her dress, and she looked down at the great, liquid eyes closing in contentment. An indescribable feeling of tenderness washed over her, and she felt the hot prickle of tears. She crooned to the horse without realising it, then remembered Rissom's presence and looked up at him with sheepish wonder.

'I think I'm in love,' she whispered.

'That makes two of us,' he smiled back, and though her heart remembered to flutter, she understood that the love they shared was for this incredible creature who had long since fallen asleep under her hands.

Charles led her quietly from the stall and pulled the sliding door closed behind them and, like parents of a child finally put to sleep, they tiptoed together out of the quiet barn.

Once outside, Valerie flung her arms wide in a luxurious stretch, as if she wanted to embrace the whole world. Failing that, she wrapped her arms around each other, hugging herself, and smiled at Charles.

'There's a bench over here, if you'd like to sit for a while,' Charles said softly.

'I'd like that. It's too beautiful a night to go back to the motel this early.'

They settled on the smooth wooden slats of a contoured bench at one side of the barn's entrance. Both of them exhaled a long, contented sigh in unison, and laughed softly together at the sound.

The bench faced the hill that sloped down through the trees to the parking area. Spiralling tendrils of the night's first fog rose up from the lowland, creating the illusion that the hill upon which they sat was totally isolated from the rest of the park, a world unto itself.

Valerie was still glowing from her experience with Sheikh, and that euphoria, coupled with the quiet peace of the surroundings, succeeded in creating a moment in time that erased all that had gone before, and ignored all that would come afterward.

'I think that was probably the most remarkable experience of my life,' she said hesitantly, afraid that verbalising the feeling would make it seem less than it was. 'I know that sounds silly,' she added lamely.

'No sillier than a grown man apologising to a horse,' he replied with a smile.

'I never thought that was foolish,' she put in quickly. 'But I didn't understand it. Now I do.'

'Good.'

He leaned back, locking his hands around one knee, and looked at a point somewhere in the distance. 'There's something special about gaining the trust of an animal more powerful than you are,' he mused. 'I feel it every time Sheikh nibbles at my hand, or butts me with his head, when he could just as easily break my bones with his jaw or strike out with his hooves. There's a demanding honesty about relating to a horse. Their trust is absolute, when they finally give it, but they'll only continue to give it as long as you earn it.'

'Like a business relationship,' Valerie chided him. 'It only prospers as long as both parties benefit.'

'Exactly. It's clean, predictable . . .'

'And it's more than that, Charles Rissom. You love that horse.'

He tipped his head sideways to look at her. He stared in deadly earnest for a moment, and then suddenly he smiled, and his whole face changed.

She shared the smile, but her voice was soft, and serious. 'Why don't you take Sheikh home?'

He sighed and shook his head. 'He's too valuable to be hidden away. I thought you understood that.'

She made a little line with her mouth and looked down. 'Well, I don't. Not anymore. It just doesn't mesh with my own idea of value, I guess.'

'And what's that?'

She looked at him thoughtfully. 'That the only things worth having are the things you want with you all the time.'

His eyes rested on hers quietly for a long moment, and then he reached out and caught a lock of her hair between his fingers. He rubbed it to a soft gloss with his thumb, then tucked it behind her ear and let his fingers drift forward to touch her cheek. His eyes followed his hand as it explored her face delicately, as if he were memorising every detail with both sight and touch. She followed his eyes with hers, breathing shallowly, quietly, for fear of breaking the tender spell with sound. When his fingers touched her lips, they parted automatically, and her nostrils flared slightly as she drew in a deep breath. He rose quickly and pulled her to her feet to face him, then cradled her head in his hands in a gentle embrace. She stood motionless before him as if she were frozen to the spot, helpless to either resist or to return the caress of his hands, pulsing under the power of his touch. He pulled his hands away briefly, as if to test his own ability to do so, and his eyes narrowed slightly as he stood apart from her, simply looking. His gaze dropped to her breast as it rose and fell quickly beneath the thin fabric of her dress, and he watched the tempo of the motion flutter and increase as if he had touched her. His hand rose to hang suspended just beneath her chin, a fraction of an inch above the full mounds rising to meet it, and when the fingers finally relented and brushed against one peak, she caught her breath and held it in her throat. His eyes found hers and held them, commanding her to look, to acknowledge, to admit his power; and her gaze was steady and open until his hand cupped her breast, then she closed her eyes and exhaled a tiny cry.

Both his hands returned to her head, where he threaded his fingers into the thickness of her hair. He held her head motionless while his lips descended to hers, and when they met, there was an explosion between them as they gasped in unison, and their mouths moved and moulded in an equal, searching union as their bodies came together. Valerie's hands moved between them to flatten against his chest, to feel the vibrant echo of her own furious heartbeat beneath his shirt. He tensed under her touch, then suddenly his hands were on her shoulders, pushing her away, holding her at a distance when every fibre of her being cried to be one with his. She held her breath as she watched his face, waiting for the rejection, waiting for him to remind her that she belonged to another man, waiting for his contempt. But he said nothing, and there was no mockery, no contempt in the eyes that narrowed and looked off into the distance.

'What is it?' she whispered.

'Listen!' he commanded with a sharp shake of his head, and then she heard what the beat of her own heart had covered: car doors slamming, the sounds of muted laughter rising up from the parking area, and the unmistakable baritone of Jacob's voice as he led the way up the asphalt walk to the barn.

Charles grabbed her arm and pulled her quickly around to the back of the barn, and they stood silently behind the cover of a honeysuckle bush in full, fragrant bloom, waiting for the small group Jacob led to pass into the barn's open doorway.

Valerie felt like a schoolgirl, hiding from the adults, concealing something tawdry and forbidden, and the feeling made her slightly ashamed. 'What are we hiding for?' she asked in an angry whisper.

Charles pressed a forefinger to his lips and replied in a low voice, 'I didn't think you'd be able to explain our presence here together to your fiancé—or did you have a lie all ready?' This time she heard the contempt creep back into his voice.

'He's not my fiancé, and you know it!' she hissed. 'That was your arrangement, not mine!'

'Maybe I was just calling your bluff,' he said coldly.

'One minute you're so . . . warm . . . so caring . . . and the next . . . ?' She shrugged again, acknowledging the question she could not answer, and turned to walk away.

'Just a minute!' he hissed, jerking her backward until she fell against him. His fingers were tight around her arm, and she felt the tension in his other hand as he grabbed her bare shoulder. Then suddenly the tension was gone, and he wrapped both arms around her from behind, crossing them under her breasts and pulling her gently back to lean against him. She stiffened slightly, resisting his coaxing arms, but then he buried his face in her hair and she felt his breath, warm and moist, just behind her ear, and her body relaxed.

There was a long, mutual silence, as if both of them knew that words could not tear down the barrier between them, and that to try would only make it stronger. She was lost in a tiny capsule of time, when the only things her senses perceived were the rush of his breath in her hair, the beat of his heart against her back, and for the moment, that was enough. But then the protective shell cracked, and she heard the muffled sound of voices from inside the barn, the grating rumble of a stall door being slid open, the sharp, authoritative sound of Jacob's voice raised in a command. She felt an inexplicable pang of regret, thinking of Sheikh being awakened, pulled from a gentle sleep to perform for the pleasure of foolish humans.

'I wish he wouldn't do that,' she m

until his thumb pressed against the base of her left breast, and then she pushed quickly away, spinning to face him while she still had the will to move.

'No,' she whispered hoarsely. 'Not again. You win. I admit it. You have the power to move me, to arouse me, to make me want you. Is that what you wanted to hear? Confirmation of your mastery? Well, there! You have it.' Her breasts rose and fell quickly with the remnants of her passion and the desperate intensity of her words, and Charles' eyes lingered on them with desire.

'I don't know what you want from me,' she continued miserably, no longer caring that she was exposing her weakness to his contempt, that her emotions would lie naked and defenceless before him. She blinked rapidly to hold back the tears. 'But I'm tired of being used. You're going to have to find someone else to amuse you.' Her voice faded and she shook her head hard, trying to pull away.

'*You're* tired of being used!' His lips pressed into a thin line, and he took a deep breath. 'Maybe it's time we practised a little honesty in our own relationship,' he said quietly.

'I didn't know we had one. What relationship is that?' she asked bitterly.

'The one we may never have.' His voice was solemn. 'Come with me.'

He took her hand and led her cautiously past the barn entrance, down the asphalt walk to his caravan. She followed meekly, afraid to go with him, but more afraid to be left behind as he walked away from her.

Once inside, he pulled heavy curtains across all the windows until she felt like she was trapped in a cave, at the mercy of its owner, then he snapped on the wall lights above the round table.

'No one will bother us here,' he said. 'Even Jacob knows I'm off limits when the curtains are pulled.'

'I wasn't worried about Jacob,' she said firmly.

'I know. That's one of the things that bothers me.'

She shivered involuntarily, and he smiled. 'Sit down. Relax. I'll make some drinks.'

Sit down, he said. Relax. The sitting part she could manage. Relaxing was something else altogether. She stopped herself from wringing her hands only by a concentrated effort, and tried to quiet the childish rolling of her stomach.

He was different, somehow—since the barn. There was a quiet sincerity in his manner, an almost hopeful deference in the way he touched her, as if he'd opened the gates, cracked the shield that concealed Charles Rissom from the rest of the world. This time she had pulled away, not trusting the integrity of his actions, fearing the rejection that had devastated her once already. Honesty, he said. He wanted honesty. But where would honesty take them? Exactly where he had said it would, if she knew him at all: to a relationship they would never have. Honesty would mean confessing that she had deceived him only for the chance to print his story, to expose him to the public and destroy the thing he valued most: his privacy. He would not forgive her that, and she couldn't blame him.

He pushed a tall, frosty glass towards her across the table, and leaned back against the counter, facing her. She fingered the glass lightly, then asked without looking up, 'What is it?'

'Grapefruit juice. A little vodka.'

She nodded without questioning that he knew exactly what she liked to drink. It would be like him to notice such a thing at the two dinners they had shared, and remember it. She tasted the drink, and gave him a weak smile of approval.

He looked at her steadily as he raised his own glass in a mock salute, then drank deeply. He set down his glass, then spoke quietly. 'It's time we talked.'

She moved only her eyes to look up at him warily, and

he smiled in spite of himself, then slid in at the table opposite her. 'You look like a puppy about to be disciplined,' he said gently. 'Is talking such a punishment?'

'Sometimes. With you, it is,' she mumbled, looking down at the table.

'Valerie.' His hand captured hers across the table and pressed it warmly. 'I've confused you, and you've confused me. No relationship thrives on deception. I meant what I said about honesty between us. Without it, there can be nothing else. So I'll practice what I preach. I'll be honest.'

She cringed inwardly, and raised her eyes reluctantly to his.

'You're one of two things,' he said steadily, tightening his grip on her hand. His eyes were riveted to hers. 'You're either a liar, or a cheat. And I don't care much for either one.'

Her eyes widened in surprise at the suddenness of the accusation, and her mouth formed an open circle.

'You claim to be Jacob's woman,' he continued sternly, 'and yet you're more than willing to fall into bed with me. That makes you a cheat.'

The muscles in her arm tightened as she tried to reclaim her hand, but he refused to let her go.

'And if you're not Jacob's woman, but only pretending to be, that makes you a liar,' he concluded harshly.

Her legs finally responded to the frantic messages of her brain, and she rose quickly, forced to lean forward across the table where he still held her hand captive.

'So which is it?' he demanded, all pretence at gentleness gone. 'Which are you?'

She hesitated, and looked directly into his eyes. 'It doesn't make much difference, does it?' she asked sadly. 'Both are equally contemptible as far as you're concerned, aren't they?'

He returned her gaze frankly, and made good on his promise of honesty. 'Probably.'

She jerked her arm with a vicious twist and reclaimed her hand, rubbing it where the pressure of his fingers had bruised it. She bumped the table as she moved towards the door, and her glass tipped and spilled its contents across the burnished wood.

His voice stopped her just as her hand reached for the doorknob. 'Doesn't your conscience ever bother you?' he asked quietly.

She turned slowly, holding her breath. 'Why would my conscience bother me?'

He looked directly into her eyes. 'For using people, like Jacob.'

'I'm not using Jacob!' she shouted.

'Does that mean you love him?'

She closed her eyes, bringing herself under shaky control. 'That's between Jacob and me.'

He jumped up quickly and grabbed her shoulders. 'And me!' he hissed. 'Because I'm the man you want in your bed, remember?' His voice lowered to an intense whisper. 'And the man who wants you, in a way Jacob could never understand. I've wanted you since the first moment I saw you, and Jacob and the rest of the world be damned! And as contemptible as that may be, at least I had more consideration for Jacob than you did. I stopped, when you were more than willing to go on. Jacob has me to thank for your fidelity!' he snapped.

'You're trying to protect Jacob?' she whispered. 'From me?'

He tipped his head back and closed his eyes. 'No,' he groaned. 'I'm trying to protect myself. Besides, after last night, after thinking about last night. I was sure you weren't Jacob's woman. That's why I did what I did tonight at the restaurant—to force you to admit that you weren't.'

'And when I didn't?'

He opened his eyes and looked down at her. 'Then I

wasn't so sure anymore. For the first time in my life, I wasn't sure,' he whispered.

She took a step forward to relieve the pressure of his hands on her shoulders and looked up at him. 'Which would be worse?' she asked softly. 'If I belonged to Jacob and still wanted you; or if I had just been pretending, and never loved Jacob at all?'

'It would depend,' he said seriously, 'on why you were pretending.'

She nodded silently, knowing he had answered her question. Her chance for a relationship with Charles Rissom was gone. She had thrown it away herself, in that first moment of choice when she elected to conceal her identity and go for the story. Now the story was all she had left.

'Valerie,' he interrupted her thoughts. 'I can't respect deception, or betrayal. You're not giving us a chance.'

She felt a brief surge of bravado, a moment when she thought it might still be possible, that if she confessed to the charade now, before permanent damage was done, he might understand. But his eyes changed her mind. They were cynical, and knowing, and reminded her that this was the man who believed only in business. Charles Rissom, the great manipulator. And he was manipulating her, she could feel it. Seducing her in the only way she could be seduced, for whatever sick satisfaction it would give him to win out over Jacob, to have her admit she didn't love him.

She took a deep breath and looked at him squarely. She was still a journalist, and this man was news. She clung to the thought tenaciously.

'Charles,' she said softly, and her face reflected the luminous sincerity of the words she was about to utter, 'I have too much to lose.'

His face was hard as he frowned at her, and then it suddenly closed. 'I understand,' he said coldly, and turned away. She moved past him to the door, and closed it quietly behind her.

His eyes squeezed shut in a spasm of disappointment. At least he had given her every chance to tell the truth, to redeem herself in his eyes. Apparently he had been wrong, and the realisation stung. She was exactly what she appeared to be—a user—and that elusive blending of spirits he thought he had sensed from her simply wasn't there.

He jerked viciously at the handle of a cabinet drawer until it jumped out of its track and clattered to the floor. He bent to retrieve the large manila folder that Robert had handed him earlier that day, and spread its contents out across the table. An eight by ten glossy photograph of Valerie stuck to the remains of her drink on the table, and her smiling face seemed to pucker as the dampness seeped through. A small sheaf of papers was clipped together beneath the photograph, soaking up the liquid as he watched. But it didn't matter. He had read them all before. They told him nothing about the woman, only about the reporter. The cold, statistical data an unfeeling computer had relayed when Robert had phoned New York for a dossier.

He was lucky Robert had recognised her, he supposed. At least that gave him a chance to spring the trap before he was fully inside. To test her integrity, to feed her that preposterous lie about being Martin Vasslar's son, to plant an irresistible journalistic coup in front of her, and hope against hope that she cared too much for him to use it. But if she did, she would pay. She would destroy herself, as well as his hopes, for no one would believe Charles Rissom was Vasslar's son, and no one would ever again believe a journalist who claimed he was. Martin Vasslar's son would see to that. He would gladly see to that—for his employer, and his confidante, and his friend, Charles Rissom.

It was a cruel test, he knew that. But she had been

cruel, too. She had deceived him for the sake of an article that would destroy his privacy, and if she used it, she would pay the consequences.

His nostrils flared as he drew in a great breath, and he smiled ruefully, thinking of the terrible hold this tiny woman had on the supposedly invincible Charles Rissom. She was undoubtedly a liar *and* a cheat, and somehow, it didn't make any difference.

He pressed the fingers of one hand between his brows, trying to erase the frown. The thought that Jacob might be involved in her deception nagged at him, but he continued to push it aside, refusing to believe that the young trainer would knowingly set him up with a reporter. Poor Jacob probably didn't even know who she was, and of the three of them, he would be the greatest victim of all. Unless she really did love Jacob. The thought cut sharply, and he narrowed his eyes against the pain.

CHAPTER TEN

'HELLO, Uncle John,' Valerie said sleepily into the phone, rubbing her eyes and squinting at the face of the travel alarm next to her bed. 'My God, is it really eleven-thirty?'

'Yes, it's eleven-thirty!' John's voice boomed through the wires.

There was a long pause as she blinked herself awake, then he asked more softly, 'Valerie? Were you asleep?'

She yawned audibly. 'Yes, I was. Sorry. It's a good thing you called. I might have slept the day away altogether.'

'You don't sound like yourself,' he said with gruff affection. 'Are you all right?'

She smiled sadly, thinking how much she had missed the sound of his voice. 'I'm fine, Uncle John. I just didn't get much sleep last night, that's all.'

'I take it that means you were up all night writing a dynamite piece for next month's *Bulletin*?'

'Oh, you'll get your story, John. More than you bargained for.'

He grunted in satisfaction. 'So the horse show turned out to be more newsworthy than you thought. What'd I tell you?'

'It's been interesting, all right. But not the horse show, John. That's only background.'

'Dammit Valerie! What are you talking about? I sent you down there to cover a horse show, and that had better be the story you come back with!'

'You'll like this story better,' she said quietly.

'Don't try to tell me what I'll like, young lady! I like it when my reporters follow orders. That's what I like!

106

Dammit, anyway,' he muttered under his breath. 'I should have known better. I should have known you'd get sidetracked by the people and ignore the business. Who did you ferret out this time? What big name pulled you away from the story I sent you to write?'

She hesitated, her eyes closed, afraid to say it aloud, knowing that once she did, there would be no turning back. She exhaled the name quickly, in a breathy rush. 'Charles Rissom.'

John said absolutely nothing for a long time. She could almost hear the wheels turning as he calculated spread, rearranged the magazine in his mind, altered the cover. 'Does he know who you are?' he asked finally. 'Is he granting an interview?'

'No.'

She heard him take a deep breath. 'All right, Valerie. This is the big one. You'll never have another like it.'

'I know that, Uncle John.'

'Then for God's sake that care, Val. The man is no one to mess with.'

He murmured a few parting words with uncharacteristic gentleness, and then he hung up.

She showered quickly, then slipped into a filmy, loose sundress that left her arms and shoulders bare. She pulled her thick brown hair into a ponytail at the top of her head, then laughed at her reflection. She would never dare go anywhere in New York City looking like this, but her appearance suited her mood. It was more than casual, it was careless, in the literal sense of the word. She looked like a young girl without a care in the world.

The thought sobered her as she reached for her sun hat, then changed her mind and tossed it on the bed. A hat would just get in the way today. She had work to do.

'Valerie!' Jacob took the hill that led up to the stallion barn at a jog, and came up behind her puffing in the heat.

'Valerie! I've been looking all over for you!'

'I just got here, Jacob,' she said with a smile. 'I slept in this morning.'

The noonday sun had already played havoc with her fruitless efforts to remain cool, and curling tendrils of hair that had escaped her ponytail clung damply to her neck. Jacob lifted one curl and leaned over to blow under it. The sensation was cooling, and tingling, and she raised her eyebrows in surprise.

'Jacob, you don't have to romance me,' she teased. 'I'm your fiancée, remember?'

He caught the trace of sarcasm and frowned down at her. 'I looked for you last night. You weren't in your room.'

'I went for a drive,' she said truthfully. 'To cool off.'

He nodded and looped his arm through hers. 'I need to talk to you,' he said without looking at her. 'I have an hour before the Parade of Stallions. Can we have lunch?'

'Just promise me air conditioning, Jacob. I'll follow you anywhere.'

Her heart wasn't in the light banter, and he seemed to sense it. His smile was tight as they walked back down the hill to the park restaurant, and he said nothing until they were seated in a relatively quiet corner, tall glasses of iced tea sweating on the table between them.

She smiled at the brilliant periwinkle eyes, and thought again what a strikingly attractive man he was. 'It's not like you to be so serious, Jacob, or so quiet. What's troubling you?'

He sighed deeply and closed his eyes. 'I want you to marry me,' he said without warning, then his eyes flew open as she began to speak, and he stopped her quickly before the words could be said. 'No! Don't say anything. Not yet. Hear me out first.'

She nodded silently, a tiny wrinkle pulling at her brow.

'I won't say I hadn't thought of it before,' he said,

looking down at the table, 'but the whole thing seemed preposterous. Jacob Lancer, married!' He shook his head incredulously, and a strand of white-blond hair crossed his brow. Valerie reached across the table to push it gently to the side, and his eyes locked on hers in an eloquent plea.

'And not just married, but married to Valerie Kipper! It's a ridiculous picture, isn't it? Small-town, midwestern horse trainer married to world-renowned, horse-hating journalist.'

She started to speak again, but he shook his head, and continued in an earnest whisper. 'But when Charles said it out loud last night, in front of everyone, all of a sudden it didn't seem so preposterous anymore. Somehow it seemed . . . possible, and almost right.'

'Almost?' she asked gently.

He shrugged one shoulder and smiled disarmingly. 'Is it ever totally right?'

'I'm not sure,' she admitted with a smile.

'All I want you to do is think about it. You have a standing proposal of marriage from Jacob Lancer, and for what it's worth, no one has ever had one of those before. If you ever want to take me up on it, I'll be there.'

Then suddenly his eyes darkened and his expression was almost stern. 'So that's one thing,' he said quietly. 'And then there's another. About Charles.'

'What about Charles?' she asked warily.

'Do you intend to mention meeting him in your article?'

'I . . . I haven't decided. Why?'

'I'm asking you not to, as a personal favour to me.'

She closed her eyes and sighed. 'You didn't betray him, Jacob. It wasn't your fault. He was the one who told me who he was, not you; and he'll understand that.'

He shook his head quickly. 'No, you don't understand. I would never betray Charles intentionally, and he knows that. It's what it would do to him if the people here found out he was Charles Smith, that's what I want to prevent.'

'And what would it do to him, Jacob?'

'He'd lose his anonymity. He wouldn't be able to come here anymore, or to any horse functions. The press would mob them all for a chance to get at him. Surely you know that.'

'Yes, I suppose you're right.'

Jacob studied her thoughtfully, his eyes pensive. 'Will you leave him out of it, Valerie?'

She put her chin in her hands and thought sadly of what a web of lies and deceptions this trip had become. 'I'll promise you this much, Jacob,' she said finally. 'I won't write a word about Charles Rissom—or Charles Smith—without showing you the copy first. Before it goes to press.' She could say that much honestly, at least. In order to keep the promise, all she had to do was send Jacob an advance copy.

He charmed her with his smile, apparently satisfied with her answer.

'Why are you trying to protect him, Jacob? You said yourself he was a hard man to like.'

He shrugged and his smile widened. 'You're the one who said I loved everybody, whether they wanted me to or not, remember?' Then his smile faded and his tone was sombre once again. 'But it's more than that. He never had it easy, Valerie. I guess I still feel sorry for the bad times he had when he was a kid.'

Valerie frowned suspiciously. 'You *know* about his childhood?'

'I ought to. I lived through it with him. We went to school together, back in Minnesota.'

Her eyes narrowed and she leaned forward across the table. 'You went to school with him?' she repeated, her voice suddenly intense.

'Sure. All twelve years. What's so surprising about that?'

She collected herself quickly and leaned back in her chair. 'Nothing, nothing at all. I just didn't realise you'd known each other that long, that's all.'

Jacob leaned against the table and spoke confidentially. 'He had a bad time, like I said. His mother took off when we were in third grade, then his father started drinking, and never stopped. Until he died, that is.'

'And when was that?' she asked levelly.

'Senior year. Just before graduation, in fact. Say, Valerie, do you feel all right? You look awfully flushed.'

She put a hand to her cheek and felt the heat of anger. 'It's just the heat, Jacob,' she said quickly. 'I think I'll stay in here for a while.'

'Maybe you'd better. It's all too easy to get sunstroke in this kind of weather.' He arched his back and stretched in his chair, bending his arm to check his watch. 'Good Lord! I've got to get back to the barn!' He rose quickly, then bent to touch her face lightly with concern. 'Sure you'll be all right?'

'I'll be fine. I'll meet you in the barn after the show, okay?'

He frowned slightly, as if doubting her words, then smiled with a little shake of his head and left. She kept her temper in check with a frozen smile until his back disappeared through the revolving door, then her tiny fist came down hard on the table. She didn't have a corner on the deception market, that was for certain. The Vasslar story was an even bigger sham than her supposed relationship with Jacob. But why? Damn him anyway! So much for the Charles Rissom code of honesty! She pressed her fingers to her temple, trying to think. Why had he lied? Why fabricate such a preposterous story? She shuddered, thinking of how close she had come to putting it in print, and the consequences if it had ever gone to press. Rissom could have sued both her and the magazine, and he would have won on all counts. Worse yet, her credibility as an investigative journalist would have been destroyed, her career ruined.

Her lips tightened with a new resolve, a new motive for the vengeance she would extract from Charles Rissom, and she pulled notebook and pen from her purse, and began to write furiously. She paused occasionally to sip from the glass of weakened tea, but for the most part, her pen flew across the paper without hesitation.

An hour later she leaned back in her chair, exhausted. But she was satisfied with her work to that point, and the writing had alleviated some of the driving anger. She sighed deeply and passed a hand over her forehead to erase the tiny lines of concentration. Then she left the cool restaurant for the furnace-like heat of the afternoon sun.

She saw Rissom from the back as she approached the outdoor ring. He was wearing a pair of brief athletic shorts that left the rest of his body bare. Although many of the afternoon crowd were similarly dressed in deference to the heat, it seemed especially odd to see Charles Rissom so scantily clad. She had never consciously thought of his body without the elegant clothing he wore so well, and there was a disturbing quiver in her stomach as she realised that it had been those legs, those arms, and that chest, pressed so close to her own body only the night before.

He leaned casually against the rail, the posture emphasising the long, clean lines of a body in superb physical condition. He looks younger, she thought, watching the hot breeze lift his black hair and toss it in a dozen different directions, almost innocent.

'You're not nearly as intimidating without clothes,' she said snidely as she came up behind him.

He turned quickly, mild surprise registering on his

face, but lingering for only a moment. 'I've often thought the very same thing about you,' he countered, smiling at the flush that crept up her face at his reminder of that first night in her room.

She leaned over the top rail of the fence next to him, and stared into the empty ring. 'When do the classes start?' she asked quickly, trying to cover her embarrassment.

He turned sideways to face her, resting his elbow intentionally close to her hand on the top bar. 'Soon,' he replied. 'Park class is first, then driving, then a speciality costume class. I'll be riding Sheikh in that one, which should account for this outfit. Sorry it disturbs you so much.' His smile widened into a grin.

'It doesn't disturb me at all! It just doesn't look like much of a riding costume.'

He laughed and moved his hand slightly until his fingers brushed against her arm. 'This isn't the costume. It's what I wear under the costume.' His voice became serious and he laid his hand frankly on her arm. 'Valerie. Look at me.'

There was an underlying plea beneath the command, and she turned her head to meet his eyes. The lines of his face were tightly drawn as he squinted against the sun, and for the first time she noticed faint shadows under the dark eyes that betrayed a lack of sleep. It pleased her to think he had also spent a restless night, but disturbed her that the simple pressure of his hand was creating such an alarming response in her body. It didn't seem to matter that his own deception was even greater than hers, that it would have cost her her career, that he had met her with contempt, then rejected her, that she could never be totally sure of how he felt about her—none of that changed her response to the simple fact of his physical presence. He still moved her, just by touching her arm.

His eyes burned into hers for an endless moment, as if

he were seeking an answer there he could find nowhere else, then he exhaled a long sigh of resignation. 'Did you sleep well?' he asked, and she knew those were not the words he had intended to say.

'Probably as well as you did,' she answered steadily, still unable to pull her eyes from his.

'Then you didn't sleep at all.' His admission surprised her, started a little bell ringing in the back of her mind, but she didn't know how to respond to it.

He averted his gaze, but increased the pressure of his hand on her arm, as if to compensate. 'Will you be at the sale tonight?'

Her eyes dropped to his hand. For some reason, she was finding it difficult to concentrate on the conversation, or the activity around her, or anything, except for the small area of her arm under his hand. All of her senses had narrowed to focus on that one point, as if she had never been aware of that part of her body in her entire life, as if it had never existed, until he touched it. 'What sale?' she asked absently.

'The ten mares.'

'What?' She blinked rapidly and lifted her head to find his eyes on her once again. 'I'm sorry,' she said blankly. 'I wasn't paying attention.'

He smiled at her eyes, wide and wondering at her own lack of control, at her ridiculous ponytail, bobbing with every move of her head, making her look like a child, at the soft sunglow on skin nearly translucent and dewy from the heat.

'At least there's one thing we can both be sure of,' he said gently. 'No matter what our differences, physically we still affect each other the same way. Neither one of us can hide the truth about that.'

'That's honesty of a sort, isn't it?' she whispered, not bothering to deny it.

'Maybe the most important kind.'

His hand dropped from her arm to rest on her waist,

and she was vaguely aware of his fingers pressing lightly against her back, while his eyes held hers. She sensed their bodies coming closer together, but didn't know if he was moving towards her, or she towards him. She watched his lips tighten, and then part, never realising that hers did the same.

And when she heard the thunder, it seemed perfectly natural that it should be there, a raucous accompaniment to the galloping of her heart and the emotions inside her, running free at last.

But it wasn't thunder. It was applause. She felt like she had been savagely jerked from a dream, and for one mortifying moment, she thought the crowd was applauding them. Her face coloured bright red, and she pulled away from his hand abruptly and looked away across the ring. The first class was trotting in from the far entrance, and she closed her eyes in relief when she realised the applause had been for the horses.

'You had no right to do that here!' she said over the noise of the crowd.

He moved closer to speak directly into her ear, and she felt his bare chest against her arm. 'To do what?' he asked hoarsely. 'To touch you? To look at you?'

'You know perfectly well it was a great deal more than that!'

He lifted her chin with one hand and turned it towards him. 'Yes, it was, Valerie. To you, and to me. But not to anyone else here. They never saw it. All they saw was two people standing at the ring together. The rest was private. Very, very private.'

Her lips parted in wonder, and she frowned. That couldn't be true. They would have to be blind not to have seen what passed between them. Wouldn't they? She glanced at the people around them, and saw every pair of eyes focused on the horses in the ring. No one was even looking at them.

He smiled down at her disbelief, and rubbed his

thumb gently across her lower lip. 'And incidentally,' he murmured, 'I had every right.'

Then he turned away and was lost in the crowd. Her eyes remained focused on where he had been for a very long time.

She stayed at the rail and watched the entire first class without seeing a thing. Someone had won, and there was a great deal of applause, but little of it penetrated her consciousness. Occasionally she glanced down at her arm where he had touched it, as if she expected to see a mark of some sort—a brand.

A child stumbled at her feet and came up wailing, and the harshness of the cry shattered the barrier her mind had sustained for so long. A concerned mother swept the child into comforting arms, and Valerie smiled at the mother's automatic display of affection, and the child's immediate, trusting response. She looked around at the crowd, and noticed for the first time all the relationships renewing themselves before her eyes. Couples with arms wrapped around each other's waists, children with trusting hands enclosed in the large, tender grasp of those who cared for them, eyes that met, and held, and said something warm between people who stood apart and let their eyes speak for them. She was surrounded by hundreds of people living the everyday moments of love and affection, people secure in relationships they understood and trusted, and she felt very much alone.

She glanced up and saw Jacob approaching, carrying two tall plastic glasses high above his head to avoid the jostling bodies around him. Like Charles, he was dressed only in shorts, and young girls in the bleachers behind her greeted his approach with adolescent squeals. He looked over her head and flashed a grin and a wink to the bleachers, and Valerie smiled at the swooning response she heard. And she couldn't blame them. He looked like a bronzed Greek god, with his blond hair lifting as he walked, his muscles rippling with the easy rhythm of his jaunty stride.

He was still wearing the brilliant smile he had bestowed on his fans in the bleachers when he came up next to her.

'You look magnificent,' he said through the smile.

She tipped her head back to look up into his remarkable eyes, and was surprised at the ease with which she returned his smile. No matter what her mood, Jacob always seemed to put her immediately at ease, and she was beginning to cherish his company.

'And you are almost blindingly beautiful, Jacob,' she smiled. 'I can't understand why I'm not madly in love with you.'

He tossed his head in the direction of the girls in the bleachers, and they caught sight of the gesture and squealed again. 'Neither can they,' he said good-naturedly. 'But maybe you will be. In time.' He was still smiling, but his eyes were serious, and for a moment, she wished desperately that she *could* fall in love with this fascinating boy-man. How wonderfully relaxing it would be, to just sit back and let it all happen, to love a man so obviously infatuated with her, with no conditions, no secrets, no dark places. It would be so easy.

He was studying her with a thoughtful frown, and she realised she had been staring. 'Sorry, Jacob. I was just thinking.'

'Were you thinking about me?' he asked seriously.

'As a matter of fact, I was.'

'Then don't apologise.' His face had smoothed into an expression of quiet reflection, and it looked so smooth, so very nearly perfect in its striking handsomeness, that it reminded her of a one-dimensional magazine photograph.

'Here,' he said, handing her a glass. 'I thought you might be ready for some lemonade.'

She accepted the glass thankfully, realising for the first time how thirsty she was. She drank deeply of the cool, tart liquid, then licked at a piece of lemon pulp that clung stubbornly to her lip. 'Ah, thank you, Jacob. You always seem to be there with exactly what I need.'

'That should be worth something,' he said quietly.

She felt her smile slip away as she looked at his face. So earnest, so open. She would always know exactly where she stood with this man. That was worth something, too.

'You're burned,' he said shortly, turning away to lean against the rail.

As soon as he said it, she felt the dry prickle of heat on her face, and knew that he was right. 'So I am,' she said. 'Do I look ridiculous?'

She tried to coax him into the light banter that made them so comfortable with each other, but his face remained stern.

'Of course not. You never look ridiculous.'

She touched his shoulder lightly. 'What is it, Jacob? Why are you angry?'

He turned his head slowly to look at her, and she felt the now familiar impact of his eyes. 'It isn't anger, Valerie. It's just . . . seriousness. It's a rare mood with me. I don't wear it well.'

There was a subdued clatter from the other end of the ring, and he turned to face it. 'The driving class is starting,' he said. 'There are only three entries. It shouldn't take long.'

He licked his lips before he spoke again. 'I saw you talking to Charles.'

'Oh?' she said lightly, not knowing what else to say.

'He has a peculiar effect on women.'

'He's a peculiar man.' She paused, exasperated that she felt so suddenly awkward. 'He told me he was riding Sheikh in the costume class.'

He nodded without looking at her. 'I don't know why he agreed to do it. Sheikh hasn't been ridden since I took him from the farm last winter.'

'Is it dangerous?' she asked lightly, but he heard the concern in her voice.

'Stallions can always be dangerous, if they aren't handled properly. Just like anything else.'

Valerie frowned, both at the words, and the hidden meaning they implied. She didn't know quite what to make of this new, sombre Jacob with the clenched jaw and the long silences. Perhaps he was deeper than she thought, more complex. Perhaps there was more to Jacob Lancer than she ever suspected, and his veneer of joviality was just as superficial as Rissom's veneer of coldness.

The periwinkle eyes seemed stern, almost forbidding, as Jacob followed the driving class around the ring with the motion of his head. She reached out tentatively to touch his forearm, and felt the long, smooth muscle tense under her fingers. His skin was hot.

'Jacob?' she said softly, and when he turned to her quickly, as if he had just been waiting for her to speak, she jerked back suddenly in surprise. His eyes flickered and narrowed, then darkened to navy blue as her hand moved up his arm. 'They all think we're engaged, don't they?' she asked, indicating the crowd with a tip of her head.

'Yes.' The word was clipped and hoarse.

'Then it wouldn't be so strange, would it, if you kissed your fiancée?'

'No.'

He made no move towards her, and dimly, in the background, she heard the announcer awarding the ribbons for the driving class. All three places were announced, and still he simply stood there, staring at her.

'Well then? What's stopping you?'

She felt a tiny flutter of anticipation as she watched the fantastic light show in his eyes. They flashed back the rays of the sun in pinprick prisms of a dozen shades of blue. When he finally grabbed her arms, the gesture was almost brutal in its suddenness, and she instantly felt the unpleasant sensation of being managed, subdued, as if there would be a contest between them instead of a union, and his dominance could not be questioned. It was a sense of a much deeper thought than what showed on Jacob's face, and for a moment, she hoped it might only have been an illusion. His lips trembled over her mouth with the intensity of his emotion, and when his lips met hers, she fought the instinct to resist, and forced her body to restrain the impulse to flee. She waited for the pulse to become a throb, for his hands and his lips to awaken a response, but there was nothing but the simple physical fact of their mouths meeting, a phenomenon that she seemed to observe from a distance, with no personal involvement at all. There was a catcall from the crowd, calling attention to their embrace, and suddenly hundreds of eyes were watching them with noisy amusement, encouraging their display with exclamations and scattered applause.

Valerie felt Jacob's response in the intensified urgency of his lips and his hands, as if the act had become a performance. Embarrassed, she tried to push him away, but he only tightened his arms around her and increased the pressure of his lips until she felt trapped, and her efforts to free herself became more frenzied. When he finally released her, she was quivering with embarrassment and anger at herself for not anticipating the public spectacle that Jacob's kiss would become. Her face was bright red, and flushed even more at the applause that followed their separation. She had only wanted to test her reactions, to satisfy the need to know that another man could move her as Charles Rissom did. But not only had the experiment failed, it had created a circus sideshow in which the audience dictated the response of the players, and she felt strangely violated.

'Way to go, Jacob!' someone hollered, and the call

was repeated from dozens of throats while Valerie wished she could sink into the sand and disappear from sight.

She turned quickly to face the ring and looked down. Jacob stood next to her, beaming. When she could finally bring herself to raise her eyes, her line of sight led across the dusty ring, up the green hill behind it, to the figure on the summit. A man in voluminous, flowing white robes sat proudly on a dark, prancing horse, and no matter how quickly the horse moved, the figure sat nobly erect, his head turned to look down the hill, across the ring, to where Valerie stood. It was impossible to distinguish features at such a great distance, but she knew from the set of his head and the long, straight line of his back that it was Charles Rissom, and that he was looking at her.

She did not need to see his eyes to know he was watching her, and he did not need to see hers. There was a tunnel of vision between them, drawing a narrow corridor of reality that began at his body, and ended at hers, and the rest of the world simply ceased to exist.

She felt the same uncontrollable tremor she had felt when he stood next to her, the same feeling she had foolishly hoped Jacob could arouse, and the feeling directed her mind to the source, demanding the focus of every one of her senses upon the man who controlled her totally, even from hundreds of feet away.

The announcer said words her mind refused to assimilate. It was just so much noise. But then the man and the horse on the hill began to move, and her eyes followed them with an intensity that could not be broken.

Sheikh cantered sideways down the hill, skittering at the noise and at the unaccustomed costume both he and his master wore. He entered the ring at a gallop, barely under control, but Charles sat the vibrant pounding easily, his gaze undistracted from the small woman who was the focal point of his attention.

Valerie was vaguely aware of the thunder of speeding hooves as Sheikh galloped around the ring towards her, but the thunder was only an echo of her heartbeat, and her eyes never wavered from the point where they would meet Charles'.

Tassels hung from the cloth bridle that seemed too fragile to hold the mighty horse in check, and his body was draped in white and gold cloth that covered all but his head and his flying tail. Charles wore a long cloak of identical fabric that flew behind him in the wind their speed created, and it was impossible to tell where the rider began and the horse ended. The cloth head-dress that covered all of Rissom's features but his eyes trailed behind like a bride's wedding veil, and as the apparition thundered past her on the rail, Valerie felt a physical impact as the dark eyes of Charles Rissom met hers.

She followed the pair around and around the ring with her eyes, never noticing the other riders that entered the dusty arena. She never heard the gasps of the crowd when two horses passed too close to one another, slender legs pounding their punishment on the ground just inches apart. She saw only one horse, and one rider, and the speed of their passes increased in time to her own shallow breathing, as if she were part of their union, her heart flying with them.

The beat of hooves shook the earth around the ring with a throbbing that touched every person there, answering an ancient, primitive call that lived within them all. And while the hooves pounded relentlessly, the riders seemed to fly above it, their myriad, dazzling costumes floating behind, blinding those who watched when metallic colours were kissed by the sun, and shot light twice as bright back into the sky.

This was the Arabian horse as he was meant to be. Pounding the sand at dizzying speeds, flying free across the baked earth with the sun at his head and the wind at

gle thing she did was
ary anymore. Every-
r been. Her hair had
gloss, her eyes were
n, and the world had
ghed out loud at her
n front of the mirror,
y of stern sophistica-

nd it pleased her that
e imagined Arabian
e billowing pants that
the transparent cape
s transported her into
dark-eyed men, and

motions as she was of
r that he would reject
had ceased to be. As
them could hide the
d after tonight,

ring

his back, carrying his master on a blinding journey of speed and light that joined the will of man and horse as one. The petty restrictions of halter and whip seemed suddenly pathetic, and Valerie knew instinctively that she had never seen Sheikh, or Charles Rissom, until this moment, when they flew by her for the last time: proud, gallant, and free.

Her heart still pounded a vibrant answer to the hoof-beats that had long since left the ring. Even the wild applause of a crowd that had shared her hypnotic wonder could not drown out the sound of her own pulse hammering in her ears. She was mesmerised by the dust that was settling in the ring before her, and Jacob's tentative touch on her arm went unnoticed. But she heard, or sensed, the approach of power behind her, and spun quickly as Sheikh danced sideways towards where she stood. Her lips were still parted in a tiny smile of wonder, and her eyes flashed darkly with suppressed excitement.

Sheikh's nostrils flared to the limits of their extension with the force of his breath, and white froth dripped from every part of his quivering body to the ground. His neck was arched tightly, his tail standing high like a warning flag, and Jacob moved quickly to stand between Valerie and the nervous stallion.

Her laugh was giddy and low as she pushed Jacob gently aside and approached the dancing hooves boldly. She found Sheikh's head with her hands and rubbed the steaming muzzle while her eyes lifted proudly in a silent greeting to Charles. He saw the salute in her eyes, and the surrender, and a quiet understanding passed between them.

Jacob watched in frowning wonder as Valerie stroked the blowing stallion's head and neck, and he moved defensively to stand beside her. She never saw him. Her eyes were locked on Charles' dark, steady gaze as he removed the draped cloth that covered his mouth. He was no more aware of Jacob's presence than she was when he finally spoke.

'A century ago, in a place where this horse belongs, I would simply reach down, lift you up behind me, and gallop away across the sands. There would be no consideration other than the fact that I wanted you.'

Jacob watched in disbelief as Valerie stood there, neither speaking nor moving, merely looking up at Charles with a pride that matched his, her eyes flashing a bright reflection of the sun, like an exclamation point after his words.

Jacob's voice was deeper than usual, louder than necessary, as if he felt he had to shout to be heard above the deafening conversation of their eyes. 'I want to marry her, Charles,' he said defiantly, wondering why he felt the need to be defiant even as he spoke.

Charles turned his head slowly, as if the pull of Valerie's eyes were almost too strong to break, and looked down on Jacob with a kindness more frightening than his wrath had ever been. 'I know you do, Jacob,' he said gently, then he turned the horse and cantered away.

CH

THERE were no mor
returned to her ro
absolutely no doub

There would be
perhaps no story on
or not she would
American Bulletin s
mind was full of oth
only, and the things
further than that, as
motion, and then ri
take her.

She would attend
auction was over,
would talk. Sh
she had
rea'

...ale with Jacob, and after the ...ne would meet Charles and they ...ne would tell him who she was, the story ...plotted to write, and the beautiful simplicity of ...ising that the story could never be as much as the man. Between the two, she had never really had a choice, she had only postponed her acceptance of what was meant to be.

She would tell him how she learned that the Martin Vasslar story was a fake, and that it didn't matter that he lied, or why he lied. Then they would laugh together at their dual deceptions, and forgive each other, because what they shared was so overpowering that their individual pettiness could not destroy it.

She hummed a tuneless melody as she showered and dressed, and stopped what she was doing occasionally to shake her head in silent wonder at her own emotions.

She had never felt so totally at peace, so confident in

She was as ~~cer~~ her own, and the old, her again was not only ~~remo~~ Charles had said, neither one of truth about their reaction to the other, an~~d~~ they wouldn't have to.

There had been a communion of hearts at the today, a blinding revelation of the spiritual union between them that made everything else seem paltry by comparison. She belonged to Charles Rissom as surely as he belonged to her, and the rest of their lives would be merely a series of incidentals that revolved around that single, inescapable truth.

Her step was light with impatience as she left the room, feeling more like a bride than she would ever feel again.

Kentucky evenings made one forgive the merciless heat of the summer days. Although the air remained moderately heavy with humidity, that very quality held the rich perfumes of flowering trees and bushes close to the ground, and one lonely tree could fill an acre with lingering fragrance.

Valerie could not see a single flower as she and Jacob strolled through the park, but somewhere close by dogwood and honeysuckle were throwing their heady perfumes into the light breeze, and the fragrance surrounded them.

They followed other small groups in a straggling, casual caravan that converged with others like it on a large, grassy area behind the information building. An enormous, royal blue tent dominated the space, with smaller, brightly coloured canvas pavilions scattered around it.

The subdued, convivial atmosphere of a southern garden party prevailed, with all in attendance dressed in semi-formal attire, clearly enjoying the first of the evening's festivities. There was a constant, merry flow of humanity as groups of people joined and mingled, then separated and moved on, only to join a new group in a different location.

Liquid refreshments were served by stern, formally dressed bartenders in two of the smaller tents, and Jacob disappeared momentarily into one of them, returning with two glasses of champagne.

Valerie toasted him gaily and insisted on buying another round herself when they had emptied their glasses. Tonight she felt like celebrating.

'You can't buy a drink here, Valerie,' Jacob chided her gently, and raised his arm to a passing waiter who immediately refilled their glasses. 'Everything is free. Food, drinks, everything.'

'Jacob, that's impossible!' She looked around the grounds in amazement. 'There must be hundreds of people here, and they're still coming. The bill would be astronomical!'

Jacob's smile was tinged with a possessive pride. 'Arabian people never do anything halfway, Valerie.

We like to think we have a certain flair, a certain graciousness, that you don't find much anymore.'

Valerie took in the scene with new interest, absorbing the rather haughty, privileged feeling one experienced rarely, when moving in those few circles which enjoyed boundless wealth. It was a feeling she had found frequently when travelling overseas, particularly to those small city-states where monarchies still flourished and were bound by an unwritten code of ostentation. But it was an atmosphere that was no longer prevalent in her own country. Not since the turn of the century had society sparkled with the dazzle of money flowing from seemingly bottomless, untaxed wells.

'How many people are invited?' she asked, and Jacob laughed.

'No invitation required,' he responded. 'Anyone who loves horses is welcome here, and they come from all over the country. Some of these people are simply tourists who have never even seen an Arabian horse. They just happened to visit the park this week and heard we were giving a party. 'Who could turn down a night of free food and drink, and a chance to rub elbows with all the famous people you'll see here?'

'Doesn't that get a bit costly? Entertaining anyone who happens to walk in off the street?'

He shook his head emphatically. 'Not at all. It's good advertising. Those same people will walk away from here tonight with the impression that the Arabian horse people are some of the most hospitable and wealthy people in the world. And they'll be right, on both counts.' He lifted his head to peer over the heads of the crowd that was building to alarming proportions around them. 'I think I see Charles over there. Will you excuse me for just a few minutes? I want to talk to him about one of the mares on the block tonight.'

Valerie stood on tiptoe to try to catch a glimpse of Charles, but could see nothing but dozens of milling bodies, all of them taller than hers. 'Go ahead, Jacob. I'll wait right here.' She didn't want to see him for the first time tonight in Jacob's company anyway. What she had to say to Charles Rissom was for his ears alone. She smiled as Jacob walked away, remembering the phrase she had heard from Charles more than once. It was private. The expression took on a new meaning when she understood his definition. More than the dark, shoddy backroads of another man's secrets, private things were his treasures, the cherished creatures and feelings too valuable to share with the rest of the world.

A waiter filled her glass again, and the champagne enhanced her already euphoric contentment. She was in love with Charles Rissom, and all was right with the world. She passed the time until Jacob's return happily observing the people around her.

'How many of her get did you see?' Charles sipped from a short glass filled with amber liquid, his eyes dark and thoughtful.

'Four,' Jacob replied. 'The last four, in fact, and every one of them was outstanding. All by different stallions. I'm telling you Charles, that mare hasn't dropped a bad foal. She's worth any three others in the sale tonight.'

'She's certainly no beauty herself,' Charles put in. 'I had a good look at her at the preview this morning, and she's probably the least attractive of the lot.'

'That's the only thing that may keep her price down, but I'm afraid even that won't help.'

'Why not?'

'Harold Perton visited the farm three days before I did. He wants her.'

Charles nodded shortly. 'That's quite a recommendation. Perton knows his horses, too. Put a ceiling on her, Jacob. What's the top dollar you'd pay?'

Jacob shook his head. 'I can't do that. I'd pay whatever I had to to get her. She's worth it.'

'I've never heard you say that about a horse, Jacob.'

'There's only one other horse in the world I feel that way about, and you own him already.'

Charles sighed and drained the last of his drink. 'Anything else before we go in? They should be starting soon.'

Jacob hesitated only a moment before blurting out, 'I meant what I said about wanting to marry Valerie. I asked her today.'

Charles looked steadily down into his drink glass for a moment, then shook it until the ice cubes spun around in a circle. 'Did she accept?' he asked without looking up.

There was a long pause before Jacob answered. 'Not yet. But she will.'

Charles raised his eyes slowly to look on Jacob's flushed, defiant features, and felt a familiar pang of paternal protectiveness. 'Do you love her, Jacob?'

The answer was too quick, and too shrill. 'Who wouldn't? She's more than you think she is, Charles. She's not like the other women I've known. Really. I think if you ever gave her half a chance, you'd like her.' He looked down at his feet and scuffed the shiny toe of one boot in the sand. 'I know she liked you,' he said softly. 'At first, anyway.'

'Why are you telling me all this, Jacob?' he asked gently.

The blond head bent with a deep sigh. 'Because of what you said to her this afternoon . . . about picking her up and carrying her away if you wanted to. She's not that kind of woman, Charles, and I know that type of remark insults her deeply.' Jacob's voice was almost petulant.

Charles tipped his head back and his mouth opened in a silent laugh. He sobered when he noticed the angry flash of Jacob's eyes. 'I'm sorry, Jacob. I wasn't laughing at you—at myself, maybe—but not at you. And if you ask your Ms Smith, I'm sure she'll tell you she wasn't offended this afternoon. I'm afraid you were watching with your eyes closed.'

'I don't think so,' Jacob replied.

'Ask her, Jacob. And think very hard about your proposal of marriage. If she accepts, run like hell.'

Jacob's mouth dropped open in complete, indignant astonishment, but Charles had already turned to walk away.

Valerie smiled as she saw Jacob returning through the press of bodies moving towards the auction tent, but his face was dark and closed, and he didn't return her smile.

'Come on,' he ordered as he grabbed her arm and pulled her into the flow of traffic. 'They're about to start. We'll have enough trouble getting to our box the way it is.'

She frowned at the heavy hand on her arm and his sudden change of mood. 'What's the matter? Didn't you get to talk to Charles?'

'Yes, I talked to him. He'll meet us inside,' he said sharply without looking at her.

'Jacob, whatever is the matter with you? Didn't he like the same mares you did?'

He stopped suddenly and turned to her with an odd expression. 'One of them,' he said with a strange smile. 'We agree on one of them.'

He led her impatiently past the bleachers already filled to overflowing, and never bothered to acknowledge the friendly calls from spectators already seated. It was unlike Jacob to ignore his audience, and Valerie glanced at him frequently, trying to analyse his mood, but his face remained dark and closed.

They approached a series of private boxes set on a tier a few feet above ground level, and Valerie looked intently for Charles, but the Rissom box was empty. Jacob led her up the three wooden steps and gestured for her to take the end seat in the first row. She swallowed her disappointment, realising that Jacob would sit between her and Charles, then shrugged it away as a minor annoyance. The auction wouldn't last forever, and her time with Charles would come soon enough.

Dusk deepened gradually into dark, and the pavilion lights flashed on, emphasising the blackness outside with their contrasting brilliance. The long, narrow runway that bisected the tent widened to an oval directly before the Rissom box, and Valerie assumed that this was where the sale horses would be presented. Her eyes strayed to the stage stretching across the entire end of the tent to her right. She raised her brows at the richness of the elaborate decorations surrounding the auctioneer's podium. Everything was draped in a blue fabric that matched the tent's colour, and the entire stage seemed to flower with plants that blossomed in bright pink and yellow. A narrow walkway came around the stage from the back, joining the runway that passed just in front of Valerie's chair.

'Is that where they bring in the horses?' she asked Jacob, but his eyes were focused across the tent and it was obvious that he never heard the question.

She followed the line of his sight until her eyes found Charles, and her face lifted with a smile that felt too large to contain, although in reality, it only touched the corners of her lips.

He was dressed all in black, and stood out in the bright colours of the people who surrounded him like a dark prince; taller, leaner, and pleasantly sinister with the brief, hard smiles he distributed like alms to those who greeted him. He rarely acknowledged anyone with much more than mild courtesy, so when he was approached by a short, stocky man in a baggy suit and a battered hat, Valerie was surprised to see him beam with genuine pleasure, and throw his arm around the man's shoulder.

'Who's Charles talking to?' she asked Jacob, squeezing his arm to make sure she had his attention.

He blew through his lips in annoyance. 'Mickey Hart. A little breeder from Minnesota. Two mares and no money. Charles gave him a free breeding to Sheikh this year.' Jacob's tone indicated hearty disapproval.

'Why did he do that?'

'Damned if I know,' he answered bitterly. 'Why don't you ask him?'

Charles broke away from the shorter man and crossed to the box still wearing the faint remnant of a smile. His eyes met Valerie's briefly, in a flickering acknowledgment of her presence, but he, too, seemed to understand that what was between them had no need of an audience, and he did not speak to her. He sat next to Jacob with a short nod in her direction, the minimum that courtesy would allow.

Jacob seemed enormously pleased to have Valerie's interest as an excuse for his first words to Charles. 'Valerie was wondering why you gave Mickey Hart a free breeding, Charles. I thought I'd let you explain it to her.' There was no mistaking the snide implication that no reason would be reason enough.

Charles lowered his brow first at Jacob, then at Valerie, but he directed his answer specifically to Jacob. 'Because Mickey Hart has a damn fine mare, and any foal she has will be a credit to Sheikh, as I've told you a dozen times before.'

'That's nonsense and you know it, Charles! Sheikh has enough foals on the ground to credit his ability as a sire already. You didn't need Mickey Hart's!'

'Maybe not,' Charles replied evenly, 'but he did.' His curt response ended the heated exchange immediately, and Jacob's face reddened with impotent anger.

Valerie was totally bewildered by Jacob's hostility, and raised a questioning brow at Charles.

'Mickey's mare came into heat late,' he explained. 'I had to postpone Sheikh's debut in the ring with Jacob and keep him home an extra week to breed her. We missed a big show, and I'm afraid Jacob took it badly.'

'A big show!' Jacob exclaimed. 'For God's sake, Charles, it was the biggest show in the Midwest. We missed fifty breedings by not being there!'

Charles' smile was tolerant. 'And you missed centre stage,' he said acidly.

Jacob's rage might have exploded if the auctioneer had not chosen that moment to test the public address system. Valerie breathed a sigh of relief as Jacob directed his attention to the stage, reluctantly swallowing his response to the insult.

After opening remarks which seemed interminable because of the high level of anticipation, the first mare was brought into the tent at an animated trot, her head high and her tail flying. The handler showed her directly before the Rissom box, and Valerie kept checking Charles' and Jacob's faces to try to assess their reaction. They were both magnificently inscrutable.

The bidding began at $50,000 and escalated rapidly to $125,000. The gavel came down hard at the precise moment the auctioneer shouted 'Sold!', and Valerie drew in a deep, amazed breath.

'It's all so fast!' she whispered to Jacob. 'And so ridiculous! How could that one horse possibly be worth $125,000?'

Jacob leaned over until his lips brushed the hair over her ear, his earlier moodiness completely forgotten. 'That particular mare is carrying a foal by last year's national champion stallion. The foal alone will bring that price easily. Essentially, the mare was free, and the price was low.'

Her eyes widened as she looked up at Jacob in disbelief, and she caught a glimpse of Rissom's amused smile.

A ring attendant in a formal black gown presented the winning bidder with a dozen long-stemmed red roses, and Valerie had to cover her mouth to keep from laughing aloud. It was the most expensive bouquet she had ever seen in her life.

She watched the presentation of the next eight mares with renewed interest, wondering what in the world set them apart to make them so valuable.

'Bloodlines,' Jacob kept telling her, 'and remember, they're straight Egyptian Arabians. There are less than two thousand of them in the entire world. Rarity means a high price tag.'

'There's only one of me,' she retorted huffily, 'and I know darn well I'd never bring these prices on an auction block.'

Charles surprised both of them by interjecting, 'That would depend on who was doing the bidding.' Jacob frowned darkly, and Valerie looked down at her hands, blushing like a schoolgirl.

The second and third mares sold for over $200,000 each, both to an obscure senator from a southwestern state whose boyish, enthusiastic response to winning the bid delighted the crowd. The next six lots sold to people Valerie had never heard of before, and it amazed her to think that there was so much wealth, and consequently power, sitting in an open-air tent on a June evening in Kentucky. The horses had been beautiful, of course, but no more beautiful than many others she had seen. It was the unbelievably high prices that left Valerie awestruck, not the animals, until the last mare was brought around from the back of the stage.

'And now, ladies and gentlemen,' the announcer intoned. 'The last offering of the evening: Bint Alshamse, translated to mean Daughter of the Sun.'

The mare stepped cautiously around the front of the stage, flatly refusing to trot into the bright lights no matter how sternly the handler commanded her. She braced her front legs against any pull forward, and only took a few tentative steps when the lead line was allowed to go slack.

'Eleven years old, ladies and gentlemen,' the announcer continued, 'and obviously unused to the glitter of the limelight, but none the less a premier broodmare. An excellent beginning for the new breeder!'

The announcer was clearly unhappy with the mare's reluctance to enter the arena, and a faint note of embarrassment entered his voice as he spoke to the handler. 'Bring her on in, now, so the crowd can get a look at her.'

There was an undercurrent of disapproval from an audience unused to horses that refused to perform, but Valerie had leaned forward in her chair, her eyes riveted on the mare, and when she took one more step forward into the bright circle of the first spotlight, Valerie gasped involuntarily.

The mare's large, dark eyes blinked rapidly against the bright light, then adjusted, and looked warily from left to right. They seemed unbelievably large against the bone white of her elegant, chiselled head, and intensely intelligent. She picked up her feet delicately, as if the sawdust beneath them were an unworthy substance for her to walk on, and moved carefully down the runway with her head high, apparently oblivious to the frustrated urgings of her handler. There were a few sympathetic chuckles from the crowd, directed kindly at the young man who was faced with the embarrassment of a horse that refused to 'show'. But Valerie could not take her eyes from the horse, and had leaned so far forward in her chair that it balanced on only its front legs.

She did not know that the mare's body was too long, that her croup was not level, that her tail was too low. She responded instead to the presence of the creature: the pride, the unmistakable mark of breeding that is an impression, not a physical characteristic; as visible in a horse as it is in a man or woman.

'Valerie!' Jacob hissed, nudging her with his elbow. 'You're going to fall out of your chair!'

Valerie never heard him, but the mare did. She

stopped dead in front of the Rissom box, and turned her head slowly to locate the source of the sound. Her eyes focused on Valerie, and she blinked once, and to Valerie it seemed to be an incredibly wise, incredibly kind eye that had met hers, and her heart ached inexplicably. The mare turned her angular flank to the box as she followed her handler back up the runway with the breathtaking dignity of a matronly monarch, and then the bidding began.

Valerie followed the mare with her eyes, and a poignant sadness pulled at her brows. It was the only time during the entire evening that she had been oblivious to the presence of Charles. But he was acutely aware of her. He had watched her with ill-concealed intensity ever since her first, tiny gasp at the mare's entrance, and now he leaned in front of Jacob to touch her arm.

'What is she worth, Valerie?' he asked her quietly, and she looked over at him as if she were surprised not to find herself alone.

'Anything,' she whispered. 'She's worth anything,' and Charles smiled.

'I told you that already,' Jacob grumbled, and Charles' smile widened.

The bidding quickly became a contest between Harold Perton and Charles, as the two men nodded at figures the audience had never expected to hear for the balky horse. Valerie could barely contain herself when she realised Rissom intended to have the mare, and had to bite her lip to keep from shouting out higher responses every time Perton overbid Charles.

Shouting bawdy cries of encouragement as the bidding climbed to $300,000, the crowd hushed quickly when Perton jumped to $350,000. Valerie swallowed convulsively and heard Jacob swear under his breath.

The two competitors bid in agonising increments of $5,000, and hundreds of spectators were mesmerised by the contest, their heads swivelling back and forth from

Perton to Charles as the bidding crept higher and higher.

When Charles nodded casually at the auctioneer's quest for $450,000, there was a gasp from the crowd, and Perton threw his battered stetson into the ring in good-natured surrender. 'All right, Charles!' he shouted. 'Take her home to Rissom!'

The audience exploded with the noisy release of a collectively held breath, celebrating the end of tension with an ear-splitting uproar. The announcer was forced to scream into the microphone to formally accept the bid, and the figure flashed on the electronic board over his head with crazy syncopation.

Jacob leaped from his chair with a whoop of delight, and vaulted over the rail to mill with the crowd pouring across the runway to the Rissom box. The only people in the tent still seated were Valerie and Charles, who sat calmly looking at one another, identical tiny smiles reflecting a private joy.

When the attendant brought over the roses to hand to Charles, he gestured to Valerie with his hand. 'They're hers,' he said quietly. 'She's the one responsible for this. By all rights, the horse belongs to her.'

Valerie accepted the roses as if they were her due, and then looked up at Charles. 'I wish I could hold you to that,' she said softly.

'You can.'

Harold Perton blustered up to the rail before the box, his face flushed and perspiring, his smile magnanimous. 'Dammit, Charles! That was the best time I've had in years!' He reached over the rail to grab Charles' hand and shook it with tireless vigour. 'Well, hello there, Missy,' he acknowledged Valerie, and though the greeting was not unkind, it wasn't overly warm, either.

Valerie smiled politely, refusing to take offence at anything tonight.

'Listen, Charles,' Perton continued in a rush, 'the least you owe me is another look at that mare. How about walking back to the sale barn with me and escaping this mob? Maybe we can talk about a deal on her first foal by Sheikh. You do speak for Rissom, don't you?'

'I do indeed,' Charles replied wryly. 'And I was going to stop at the barn anyway. I'll meet you outside in a few moments, Harold.'

Valerie wanted desperately to go along, but as she watched Perton's broad back retreat through the crowd, she realised that now was not the time. Not yet.

Charles leaned back in his chair and studied her thoughtfully. She felt his eyes on her, and when she turned to meet them, she was lost again in that peculiar, magical illusion that seemed to isolate them from the rest of the world. The tent, the crowd, the noise, everything around them disappeared, and she and Charles were alone, just as they had been at the ring that afternoon.

His eyes roamed over her face, and then down her body, as if he were memorising every line, every curve, and she felt a rosy warmth wherever his gaze lingered. It was an extraordinarily intimate study, taking place as it did in the company of hundreds, but neither of them were aware of the presence of others.

He frowned suddenly, and his face reflected an internal struggle she didn't understand. His dark eyes fastened on hers with a brutal, questioning intensity, and her brow quivered in a frustrated response.

It didn't matter that she reached out with her hand to touch his face, to try to erase the trouble that pulled at his mouth and joined his brows. There was no one to notice her fingers trembling at his cheek, moving up to brush lightly at his frown. His eyes closed tightly under her hand, then he grabbed at it with astonishing swiftness and brought her palm up to his mouth. His face tightened as he pressed his lips tenderly into the soft hollow, and his expression was pained as he released her hand and stood quickly.

'I have to leave now,' he said hoarsely, and the sadness lingering in his eyes bewildered her.

Her sigh was ragged with disappointment, but endlessly patient. She had waited this long, she could wait a few minutes more. 'I know,' she smiled up at him. 'But it won't take forever.'

'No. It won't take forever.'

He crossed the tent rapidly, the crowd parting before the rush of his exit, like receding waves. Valerie watched until the bodies filled in the empty wake behind him, then left her chair for the obscurity of darkness outside the tent.

Jacob found her a few moments later, and pressed another glass of champagne into her hand, relieving her of the bouquet of roses.

'The crowd is crazy tonight!' he said breathlessly, touching his glass to hers in a careless toast, spilling a little of the contents on his hand. His eyes sparkled with excitement and he paced in place with nervous energy. His hair had been ruffled by the light breeze and hung in disorder across his eyes, a bright contrast to the rich bronze of his face. She reached up and pushed it gently to one side in an affectionate gesture.

'Honestly, Jacob! You're just like a little boy!' she smiled.

He became suddenly stern and frowned down at her. 'I'm trying, Valerie. I'm really trying,' he said earnestly.

She gazed up at him in puzzlement. 'Trying to what?'

'To be more serious, more . . . dignified.'

'What on earth for? Why would you want to do that?'

He looked down at the ground and mumbled, 'So I'll be more like the kind of man you'd marry.'

Her lips parted in surprise, and she looked at his bowed head tenderly. 'Oh, Jacob. That's not how it works.' She reached up with both hands to pull his face down to her level and kissed him impulsively on the cheek. 'Don't you see? You only want to marry me because I'm the kind of woman you *think* you should want. But you don't, really. You said it yourself: I intimidate you.'

'I'm learning to live with that. I could make it work,' he said in quiet desperation.

'No, you couldn't,' she said kindly. 'You'd spend all of your time pretending to be something you aren't, and you'd be miserable.'

She sighed deeply and rubbed at the tiny wrinkle between his brows with her thumb. 'You don't pick out someone you think you should love, then change to suit them, Jacob. The woman lucky enough to marry you is going to love you for exactly what you are, and from what I've seen so far, you have a choice from a cast of thousands.'

He raised his head and looked at her sadly, and the startling, beautiful eyes made her shake her head with a rueful smile. 'Dammit, Jacob,' she said softly. 'You are so impossibly beautiful. Why weren't you the one?'

The sadness disappeared instantly, and his grin was so sheepish, so typically Jacob, that she burst out laughing.

'Admit it, Jacob! You're relieved!'

He shrugged non-committally, then threw an arm across her shoulder in easy, natural companionship. 'I still love you, you know,' he insisted, squeezing her against his side.

She snuggled her head against his shoulder affectionately. 'And I love you, Jacob. In just exactly the same way.'

They moved through the crowd with a new, mutual contentment, enjoying fully the gaiety of the surroundings and the happy babble of hundreds of voices raised in celebration. They sampled bits of everything from the many tables burdened with a wide range of foods, and Valerie finally groaned in protest as Jacob dangled a boiled shrimp before her mouth.

'Not one more bite!' she groaned. 'Take it away,' and

he popped it into his mouth with a grin. His capacity for food, like his capacity for drink and merriment, seemed boundless.

The atmosphere became increasingly festive as the night wore on, with small, intimate groups gradually joining to become large, boisterous ones, and remarkably, Jacob seemed to be part of them all. The champagne flowed as freely as the spirit of fellowship, and Valerie was enjoying herself so thoroughly that the time passed quickly. It was only when someone mentioned that it was past midnight that a tiny worry line appeared on her brow. Even taking into account Harold Perton's love of conversation and Charles' devotion to business, he had been gone too long.

She clung stubbornly to the same glass she had been carrying for an hour, her eyes furtively searching the flow of humanity around her.

'Who are you looking for?' Jacob asked finally, puzzled by her increasing restlessness in the midst of such gaiety.

'Charles,' she replied absently, standing on tiptoe to peer over the turban headdress of the woman next to her.

'Oh, he's gone,' Jacob said casually, raising his glass to a passing acquaintance.

There was a hollow, empty feeling in the pit of her stomach that hadn't been there a moment before. The air seemed suddenly warm, the noise intolerably loud. She clutched frantically at Jacob's arm and pulled him to face her. 'Gone where?' she asked quickly, and although she tried to keep her voice light, the words were clipped and intense.

Jacob frowned slightly, momentarily put off by her expression. 'San Francisco, I think. His plane left . . .' he paused to consult his watch, '. . . almost an hour ago. Why?'

She released his arm and dropped her eyes to stare

blankly into the distance. She saw nothing, she felt nothing, except for a slow, creeping numbness that made its way from the soles of her feet to the top of her head, leaving her absolutely empty.

Jacob shook her gently by the shoulder. 'Valerie? Valerie, what is it?'

'Nothing,' she responded dully. 'Nothing at all. I . . . didn't have a chance to say goodbye.'

'Oh, that!' Jacob's smile was relieved. 'I'll give him your best when I see him, don't worry.'

He was immediately distracted by the bellowed greeting of a man lurching up to them, and never noticed Valerie walking slowly away across the grounds.

The party noise receded behind her as she made her way through the park up to the stallion barn, and by the time she stood in front of Sheikh's stall, she could barely hear the faint tinkle of laughter carried by the evening breeze. The stallion nickered a sleepy greeting as she slid open the heavy door and walked up to his head. Her arm looked pale and tiny as she wrapped it around the great, dark neck, and she stroked his muzzle gently with her other hand.

'So,' she whispered into his mane; 'he left you too, eh boy?'

Then she began to cry.

Hundreds of miles away, 20,000 feet over the flat, dusty Nebraska plains, Charles Rissom sat alone in the spacious cabin of his private jet. It had taken every ounce of will he had to leave, and even now, he wasn't convinced he had done the right thing. But he had to know. She had left him no choices.

She was free, now, to make her own decisions— whether or not to marry Jacob; whether or not to destroy Charles Rissom—and what she decided would tell him everything he needed to know about Valerie Kipper. All he had to do was wait. And as he'd said, it wouldn't take forever. It would only seem that long.

CHAPTER TWELVE

'HERE. I've warmed you a brandy.'

The firelight danced through the heavy glass of the snifter as it hung momentarily between their hands.

Valerie was curled on the floor directly in front of the fireplace, and smiled up her thanks as she accepted the glass.

'Thanks. This will make the evening perfect, Uncle John.'

He eased his stocky frame into the armchair that faced the fire and stretched his legs out in front of him. 'I doubt that,' he rumbled. 'Nothing's been perfect for you since Kentucky.'

'Don't start that again, please.'

'Don't start?' he boomed. 'It never finishes! You've done nothing but mope around ever since June!'

She suppressed a smile at his usual exaggeration, and winced at the decibel level of his voice. 'John, I've been to Washington, England, and South Africa since I got back from Kentucky. I'd hardly call that "moping around".'

He muttered under his breath and shifted awkwardly in his chair. 'You know what I mean,' he mumbled, and she sighed deeply and moved back to lean against his chair.

'Yes, Uncle John. I know what you mean.'

'So call him, dammit! Write to him! Do something!'

'No!' she said more sharply than she had intended. 'Besides, I couldn't if I wanted to. No one knows how to reach Charles Rissom. Not even you.'

The truth of the remark stung him, and he screwed up his mouth in exasperation. She was right, of course. No one could reach Charles Rissom unless he wanted to be reached. God knows he'd tried.

She tipped her head back against his knee, and he began stroking her hair absently. 'I want you to be happy, Val,' he said softly, and she chuckled at the timbre of his voice. Whenever John tried to sound gentle, the words always came out sounding like Billy Goat Gruff on one of the records she'd listened to as a child. It still made her laugh.

'I am happy, Uncle John. Or at least I'm getting there. It just takes time.' She reached over her shoulder to pat his knee affectionately. 'I have a fabulous career, lots of friends, and a doting uncle. What more could anyone want?'

He grunted sceptically and satisfied himself by staring into the fire, reflecting over the last three months.

He had barely recognised her when she returned from the disastrous Kentucky assignment. Her physical appearance had been the same, of course, but she was stone-hard and uncommunicative, and had locked herself away for days while she worked on the Rissom story.

He had been so anxious for the story himself that he never questioned her absence from the office or the dinner table, and refused to intrude during her days of self-isolation. He remembered the addictive frenzy of working on a big story from his own days as a young reporter, and waited patiently for her to finish. When she appeared in his study a week later, he beamed with anticipation until she got close enough for him to see the deep shadows under her eyes and the sunken hollows in her cheeks.

'Good God, Valerie! What's happened to you!' he had shouted. He had poured her a brandy that night, too.

She had tossed a sheaf of papers onto his desk, saying simply, 'Read it,' and when he had finished he shook his head and emitted a long, low whistle. The story was

dynamite, exposing Rissom's secret identity as Charles
Smith, touching on his troubled childhood, detailing a
streak of hardness in the man who disdained the very
people he dealt with. But it had been more than that,
too. There was a subtle undercurrent throughout the
story that painted a softer picture of the mysterious
Charles Rissom, and though the average reader might
never have seen it, John turned over the last page with a
strange reluctance to invade the man's privacy. Valerie's
writing had done that, not the story itself, and John saw
through the thin veneer of her silence immediately.

'You love this man,' he had said in wonder, and
Valerie had picked up the story and tossed it into the
fire.

'I just wanted you to read it first,' she had said. 'But I
can't let you print it.'

She had expected him to scream and rant at her
destruction of the story, and when he didn't, the veneer
cracked completely. She had cried in his arms for nearly
an hour, and told him everything. It had been all he
could do to fight back the anger, and the evening had
ended with Valerie trying to quiet him, instead of the
other way around.

He smiled now, remembering those first weeks. She
attacked every assignment he gave her like a demon,
begging for those that would send her away, the farther
the better. And her reporting had been excellent: better
than she had ever done, in fact. Cold, incisive, and
absolutely objective. Rumour had it she'd win a Pulitzer
nomination for her report on the South African story,
but even that news hadn't excited her. She remained
aloof and remote from personal involvement in anything, be it work or friendships, and John longed for the
hot-tempered, emotional Valerie she had been before.
She still had fire, there was no denying that, but it was a
cold fire, with no compassion, no humanity, and sometimes her new hardness frightened him.

She received occasional calls from Jacob Lancer, and though she seemed artificially bright in the conversations he had overheard, the mood vanished the moment she hung up the receiver. John had answered the phone once when Jacob had called, and demanded to know how he could reach Rissom.

'I beg your pardon, sir?' Jacob had asked respectfully.

'I said give me Rissom's number, dammit!' John had thundered.

'You're Valerie's uncle, aren't you? The editor. I'm sorry, sir. I can't give out Mr Rissom's telephone number.'

'The hell you can't! I won't publish it, man! I just want to talk to him about . . .'

But Jacob had hung up quietly before John could explain. He hadn't called since.

'You're awfully quiet, Uncle John,' Valerie murmured at his knee. 'What are you thinking about?'

He stirred in his chair and patter her head. 'Nothing. Everything. This month's *Bulletin*. What else?'

'You're lying,' she yawned. 'There isn't anything in this month's *Bulletin* worth thinking about. It's a dull issue.'

'Your story on the Egyptian Event is in there. That's hardly nothing.'

'Compared to what the story might have been, it is,' she said drily.

John grunted his disagreement. 'The readers will never know they missed a story on Charles Rissom. They'll be titillated enough by Charles Smith and his cool bidding at the auction.'

She stretched her arms out wide and straightened, arching her back. 'Maybe. Did it go out today?'

'Yesterday, Valerie,' he scolded. 'Today's the 29th. Good Lord. It's almost October.'

She stood slowly and stooped to touch her fingers to the floor, flexing the kinks out of her legs. 'And tomorrow's a workday. I think I'll turn in. Shall I get you another brandy before I go up?'

He smiled up at her and shook his head. 'Good brandy should never be drunk in a room with less than two people . . .'

'. . . or more than two people,' she finished. 'I know.' She bent and kissed the balding spot on top of his head. 'See you in the morning, Uncle John.'

Valerie climbed the curving staircase tiredly, exhausted by the pretence of casual conversation with her uncle. She didn't know why she bothered to pretend with him, anyway. He always saw right through her.

But she was getting better. Every day it got a little easier. Admitting it had been the hard part. Once she got past that, she felt the healing begin. So he didn't love her. So there had been nothing between them at the ring that afternoon, or at the auction that evening. She had imagined it all. Those long, dark looks had been nothing but long, dark looks. So what? People had their hearts broken every day, and most of them managed to pick up the pieces and carry on. She could certainly do as well, given time. But did it have to take so damn long?

It had already been three months: three agonising months of jumping every time the phone rang, of forcing her heart to slow down whenever she heard a voice like his, or saw someone with the same black hair, the same long, lean build. She smiled ruefully as she watched her feet on the stairs. Slowly, she thought. One step at a time.

She had followed a man for over five blocks one day, and that had been only last week. And you think you're getting better, she chided herself. The man had been standing outside her office building just as she left work, and she caught a glimpse of an angular face that stopped her breath in her throat. Everything about him had been achingly familiar: his height, his hair, even the set of his head as he walked rapidly away. She had followed him through the weaving rush hour crowds until it finally occurred to her she was on a fool's errand, even if the man did turn out to be Charles. What could she say to him? What could she possibly say to a man who clearly did not want her?

She shuddered, remembering her foolishness, and made her way down the wide, upstairs hallway to her room. Work was the answer; the magic panacea. And tomorrow morning she could go to work again. All she had to do was get through the night.

The nights were very hard.

'Well, here's the day's good news, Val.' Margaret lay a foot-thick stack of mail directly in the centre of Valerie's desk.

'Oh, Margaret,' she moaned. 'Give me a break. It's the first day on a new issue. Can't we just burn this stuff?'

Margaret wagged a plump, maternal finger and shook her head solemnly. 'That's no way to talk about letters from your fans, young lady, although I must admit you do look like you could use a break from this grind. You're too thin, and too pale. Have you talked to that tyrant uncle of yours about a vacation?'

Valerie smiled up at the older woman with affection. 'The tyrant uncle has been trying to get me to take some time off for months, Maggie. Why don't you marry him and get him out of my hair?'

'I fully intend to,' Margaret proclaimed with a lift of her chin. 'Just as soon as he's old enough.'

Valerie shook her head and smiled. Margaret and Uncle John had loved each other ever since Maggie took the job as his secretary three years ago, and promptly bullied him into submission. Both single for most of their lives, marriage frightened them equally. But they were working up to it.

'Well, what's in this mess, Maggie?' Valerie smacked

the pile of papers with one hand, anxious to be rid of it. 'Anything important?'

'Like I said, fan letters, most of them. They're on the bottom. A nice letter from the Japanese consul you interviewed, confirmation of your appointment in Washington next week, and scads of invitations.'

'Did I accept any?'

'As a matter of fact, almost all of them. Except the one to speak at your high school reunion next month . . .'

'Oh, spare me!'

'. . . I did, and another from some crazy in Minnesota, of all places.'

Valerie stiffened slightly, but her voice was casual. 'Minnesota? I received an invitation from Minnesota?'

Maggie chuckled. 'Not just Minnesota, mind you, but a *farm* in Minnesota. Can you imagine? I almost threw it away, but . . .'

'Who was it from, Maggie? What was the name?' she asked quickly.

Margaret frowned at her sudden interest. 'Good heavens, I didn't pay any attention to . . . or come to think of it, I do remember. It was a cable, for one thing, and that was unusual . . .' she began sorting through the stack of letters, '. . . and the name was so common, obviously a fake . . . let's see, Smith. That was it. Ah! Here it is. Charles Smith.'

Valerie snatched the flimsy yellow sheet from Margaret's hand and pulled it close to her face. Her fingers were trembling so violently she couldn't hold the paper steady enough to read, and she finally set it down on the desk in front of her.

It was addressed to Valerie Kipper, Investigative Journalist, care of the magazine. So he knows who I am, she thought.

'Valerie, for heaven's sake! You're as white as a sheet,' Margaret worried aloud. 'Who the devil is this Smith character anyway?'

Valerie tore her eyes reluctantly from the cable and frowned at Maggie's expression of concern. 'I'm sorry, Maggie. I didn't mean to be rude. It's personal, that's all.'

'Hmph. It didn't sound too personal to me.'

Valerie touched Margaret's arm lightly, pushing her gently in the direction of the door. 'Ask Uncle John,' she said. 'He knows all about it.'

'I may just do that,' she frowned, and closed the office door softly behind her as she left.

Valerie closed her eyes briefly in silent preparation, and then read slowly, never wanting the words to stop. It didn't matter what they said, not at first, it only mattered that they were from Charles.

SAW STORY ON EGYPTIAN EVENT STOP COME TO MINNESOTA FARM FOR STORY YOU MISSED STOP EXCLUSIVE ON C.R. STOP TICKETS TO FOLLOW STOP CHARLES SMITH STOP.

She became perfectly still. For an instant that seemed to stretch into eternity, she stopped breathing, stopped thinking, and felt her heart hang suspended between beats. The faint clatter of the electronic typewriters in the outer office seemed to grow louder and louder in the sudden quiet of her mind, and when the noise became unbearable, she finally breathed again.

She read the cable over and over until her vision blurred, and the only word that jumped out of the mist was STOP, like an ominous portent of unsuspected danger.

She shook her head angrily, collecting the thoughts her emotions were scattering like ashes in the wind. Get hold of yourself, Valerie, she commanded silently. Think it through. Think it all through.

He knows who you are—Valerie Smith is dead, long

live Valerie Kipper—so Jacob obviously told him everything. Including the fact that you were never Jacob's mistress. Could it be that Jacob just told him? Was that all he was waiting to hear?

She clung to that possibility desperately for a fraction of a second, then her face fell as she remembered her last telephone conversation with Jacob. He had seen Charles only once, shortly after the Egyptian Event, and they'd had a disagreement of some sort. He hadn't spoken with him since, Jacob had told her, and didn't intend to until he returned from Egypt. October fifteenth, she remembered. Jacob said he would arrive back in the States on October fifteenth. He must have told him in June, months ago. Charles had known all that time that she had never belonged to Jacob, and yet he had never tried to contact her.

She sighed heavily and pushed herself away from the desk. So much for the theory that Rissom had only rejected her because of her relationship to Jacob. She was right back where she started from. The cable hadn't changed a thing. Her memory tugged her back to all the relationships she had ended when the men became too serious. Had she left them with the same emptiness she felt now?

She flicked at the corner of the cable with one finger, and her forehead creased in thought. So why the invitation? It was so deceptively simple, so perfectly logical, just like the man himself, that the reason had almost escaped her.

She was being rewarded. He'd read her story, appreciated that she hadn't blown the whistle on him, and in his own superior way, he was grateful. Charles Rissom was patting her on the head. Nice of you, Valerie, to keep your mouth shut. In exchange, I'll give you the exclusive on Charles Rissom, American Man of Mystery.

Her mouth twisted in a wry grimace, remembering the agony of choosing between the story and a relationship with the man. In the end, she had opted for the relationship, and now, ironically, he had rejected the relationship and was offering her the story. God, life was funny. It just never stopped being funny.

She began to laugh, quietly, at first, then harder and harder until her face was wet with hysterical tears and her stomach ached, and this was the way John found her.

She sobered immediately when he barged in without knocking, and blinked her moist eyes rapidly at his ominous countenance. But then he stomped over to her desk like an angry thundercloud with legs, and even the rage on his face seemed funny. Everything did. She began to giggle uncontrollably, and pressed a hand to her mouth to hold the unseemly noise inside.

'What's this Maggie tells me about an invitation from Charles Smith?' he demanded gruffly, and Valerie giggled again.

'It's true, John,' she smiled. 'It seems that the almighty Charles Rissom is handing us the story of his life on a silver platter. As a thank-you, you might say, for not printing it in the first place.'

It didn't seem quite so funny when she said it out loud, and her smile twisted slightly.

John merely nodded.

'I've even been invited to the secret hideaway,' she continued flippantly, 'and that in itself is such an honour that I'll probably be expected to kiss his ring when I arrive.' She heard the bitterness in her own voice, and dropped her head, embarrassed to be so superficial.

'Nothing else?' John asked harshly.

She made a face and tossed the cable across the desk. 'Here. Read for yourself.'

John read the cable, then crushed it into a ball and threw it across the room. 'Bastard!' he hissed vehemently, and Valerie's face softened at his hostile defence of her emotions.

'He really isn't,' she put in softly. 'You'd have to know

him to understand how generous this gesture really is, and how much it cost him to make it.' She hesitated, and closed her eyes. 'It isn't his fault that he doesn't love me, Uncle John. It's unreasonable to hold that against him.'

'Speak for yourself!' he muttered.

'John, it's the chance of a lifetime. The only interview ever, with a man the press has been trying to reach for years. And he's willing to trust us with his story. Give him credit for that much, at least.'

'Do you mean to tell me you're actually going?'

'Of course I'm going. It's a story, and I'm a journalist.'

John pursed his lips and shook his head sadly. 'After what he did to you . . .'

Valerie clucked her tongue in exasperation. It was hard enough to have to deal with this privately; having to explain it to someone else was agonising. 'He probably isn't even aware of doing *anything* to me, John, and I'm certainly not going to give him the satisfaction of finding out. Not accepting this assignment would just be an admission that I can't get over him, don't you see? I'm not fool enough to think it isn't going to be painful, but I am going. Call it therapy, if you like, getting back on the horse that threw you, whatever. It's something I need to do. Understand?'

John grimaced doubtfully. 'I just don't want to see you get hurt, that's all.'

She walked over and wrapped her arms around his ample middle. 'My guard is up this time, Uncle John. Charles Rissom won't hurt me again.'

CHAPTER THIRTEEN

THE jet touched down lightly at Minneapolis-St Paul at nine-ten the following evening. Valerie heaved a deep sigh of relief to have survived one more flight intact, and deplaned as quickly as possible.

As she hurried through the monstrous umbilical cord that connected the airplane to the terminal, she wondered how Charles would greet her, and if she looked as terrible as she felt.

The tickets had arrived by special messenger moments after her conversation with John, and it was only then that she learned she had just one day to pack and rearrange her schedule. His presumption had irritated her. He apparently assumed that she'd be more than willing to drop everything and rush to meet his convenience, as if he were the only person in the world with anything of importance on his calendar. She had almost decided not to go right then, and having to rush through preparations to leave had done nothing to improve her mood.

She was furious by the time she finally boarded the plane, but had mellowed during the long, smooth flight. Her fear of flying was partly responsible, as was her fear of seeing Charles again. The closer they flew to Minneapolis, the more reticent she became, and by the time they touched down, she was almost cowering in fear of her own reactions.

I can take it, she had told John as she left. She recalled the words with a rueful smile, and bravely scanned the departure gate for the figure of a man she had longed to see for months.

'Good evening, Ms Kipper. I trust your flight was pleasant?'

She could barely conceal her astonishment at seeing Robert, the obsequious waiter from her Lexington motel. 'Well! Robert, wasn't it? Whatever are you doing here?'

'Why, I'm here to fetch you, Miss, of course.'

'To fetch me? I don't understand . . .'

'Mr Rissom sends his apologies for not meeting you personally. He was called away unexpectedly.' He touched his cap with polite deference. 'If you'll give me your claim tickets, I'll collect your luggage so we can start back. It's rather a long drive, I'm afraid.'

She scrambled in her purse for her baggage claims, looking up periodically with a puzzled expression. 'Did Mr Rissom hire you in Kentucky, Robert?' she asked finally, unable to contain her curiosity.

He smiled and brushed at an imaginary speck of lint on the sleeve of his spotless uniform. 'I've been with Mr Rissom for seven years,' he said with some pride. 'I travel with him frequently, and serve in a variety of positions when we're on the road. Waiter, chauffeur, secretary . . .'

'I see,' she said coolly. 'Bartending is just one of your many talents.'

'Thank you, Miss. Shall we go?'

She followed Robert's ramrod-straight back through the terminal, feeling uncomfortably like a fool for not realising he was an employee of Rissom's. It made her painfully aware of how very little she had really known about the man, and for some reason, that knowledge was embarrassing. How childish she had been to think she knew Rissom's heart, when she didn't even know who his employees were!

She tried to shrug off the irritation that Charles hadn't met her at the airport himself, recognising it as just another foolish expectation. She simply wasn't important enough to justify the sacrifice of his precious time. Remember who you are, she repeated to herself over and over. You're Valerie Kipper, reporter, and he's Charles Rissom, assignment. Nothing more. Be cool, be pleasant, be professional, and you'll be able to handle this, and he'll never know. She climbed obediently into the back seat of the limousine, fortified by her indignation, and ready for the first time to meet Charles on his own, arrogant level.

Robert guided the long car through a series of complex cloverleaf exchanges before settling on a relatively empty freeway leading north. When he no longer seemed distracted by the last vestiges of outward-bound traffic, Valerie attempted conversation by asking how long it would take to get to the farm.

'It's about an hour from here, Miss. If you'd like music, the controls are in the panel to your right.'

His formality negated any thoughts she had of questioning him about his employer, and she sagged back against the plush seat and allowed herself to doze.

She wakened to the sound of gravel crunching under the tyres an hour later, and peered sleepily out the side window. There was little to see in the blackness of the overcast night, except that the car was negotiating a narrow drive flanked by thick shrubbery of some sort. Little pinpoints of light flickered through the trees ahead, and she leaned forward with interest.

Robert noticed the movement in the back seat and spoke softly. 'It's really lovely in the daylight. It's a shame that your first look at the place had to be at night.'

She sensed a warm undercurrent of homecoming in his voice, and smiled at him through the rearview mirror. Somehow she never thought of rigidly proper people like Robert calling any place home, and the revelation made him seem a little more human.

'Here's the main house now,' he announced, and

Valerie turned her head to the window and gave a tiny exclamation of delighted surprise.

It was not the glass-and-stone mansion she had expected, with exterior lines as hard and severe as the man himself, but rather a massive, sturdy Dutch Colonial with warm, grey siding and sparkling white trim. The back of the house seemed to disappear in the shroud of darkness, and she could barely discern its size, but an old-fashioned, open front porch wrapped around the front of the structure like an old woman's skirts, and charmed her immediately.

'Why, it's lovely!' she whispered. 'And not like Charles Rissom at all!'

It was the first time she'd heard Robert laugh, and the mellow warmth of the sound surprised her as much as the house had. He stopped the car at the side of the great house, and turned to smile at her over the back of his seat. 'I think in time, Miss, you'll find that the house is very much like Mr Rissom. Very much indeed.'

Valerie stepped out of the car and breathed deeply of the warm, night air, not yet sharp with frosty warning of winter, but cleaner, crisper than summer's heaviness. She walked around to the front of the house while Robert busied himself with her bags, and admired the solid lines of the spacious porch, thinking how incongruous the setting was for a cold man like Charles Rissom. An old courting swing hung from chains at one end, creaking slightly in an unseen wind, and though she could imagine herself seeking the relief of a summer night's breeze in just such a swing, she could only picture Charles in the cool sterility of an air-conditioned room.

The double doors centred in the porch suddenly opened wide, and a path of warm, golden light escaped the house and fell on Valerie as she paused at the bottom of the steps.

'Well, come in, child! Don't wait for Robert or you'll be out there half the night!'

The wide doorway was almost blocked by the woman's ample frame, and Valerie smiled involuntarily at the scolding, maternal tone in her voice. She trotted up the steps obediently, and grinned shyly at the rosy, round face of a woman she decided to love on the spot. 'Hello,' she said breathlessly, feeling like a child in the presence of someone's benevolent grandmother.

'And hello to you, Valerie Kipper. It's high time you crossed this threshold. Come in, come in!'

She bustled Valerie through the door, then poked her head back out to scold Robert. 'Now don't dally! The coffee's hot right now, and I have a light supper all laid out,' she called.

Robert's dignified reply was lost in Valerie's smug laughter. Hearing anyone bully the ever-so-prim Robert was a treat worth the trip in itself. She wondered how he responded to the gentle bossiness of this motherly tyrant.

'Well now!' The woman closed the door and brushed her plump hands together. 'Would you like to go straight to your room, or will you have something to eat first?'

'I think I'd like something to eat,' she replied instantly, a little surprised at her sudden appetite.

'Good! I can't stand to see people go to bed on an empty stomach.'

I'll just bet you can't, Valerie thought with secret amusement. I can see you making cocoa and serving warm cookies right off the sheet, and wringing your hands if someone eats less than three of anything. That this woman was somehow connected with the life of Charles Rissom was more surprising than the house itself, and Valerie stifled the uncomfortable feeling that she had been taken to the wrong place altogether.

'I'm sorry to be rude,' she said suddenly, 'but who are you?'

The gentle face fell into an expression of horrified dismay, and the woman pressed one hand to her cheek.

'Oh dear. I am sorry. I'm Mrs Willers, but everybody here calls me Willy. Well, not everybody. Robert calls me Mrs Willers, of course.'

He would, Valerie thought to herself.

'I run the house,' she continued brusquely, 'manage the help, and do most of the cooking. I'm not sure what that makes me. We never have figured out a title for it.'

Valerie shook her head with a disbelieving smile.

'What's the matter, child?'

'I just can't imagine you working for Charles Rissom, that's all. You're not exactly . . . what I expected. None of this is.'

She waved her arms to indicate the surroundings, and Mrs Willers smiled tolerantly. 'I imagine you have more than one surprise coming from Charles,' she said gently, and Valerie marvelled at her tender reference to her employer. 'Now you just make yourself comfortable. I'll have the table laid in a jiffy.'

She disappeared through a wide door with surprising agility for a woman of her size, and Valerie turned in a slow circle to examine the room.

A merry fire crackled in a fieldstone fireplace that dominated one end of the long room. The furnishings spoke of quality and craftsmanship, but the cozy groupings and the muted fall colours made it all seem very casual. She could see Mrs Willers' touch everywhere she looked, from the mixed bouquet of autumn flowers on the glass sofa table, to the high gleam of polish on every piece of wood. It was the kind of room that made you want to kick off your shoes and stretch out on the floor by the fire, and certainly not the kind of room in which she would ever expect to see Charles Rissom.

Robert came through the front doors with her bags, looking just as stiff and formal as ever, and strangely out of place in the country house.

'If you'd care to follow me now, Miss, I'll show you your room before supper,' he said with a nod, and led her up a broad, curving staircase that bisected one end of the long room.

Her bedroom sprawled across at least one-fourth of the entire second floor, and although there was no flagrant ostentation, every detail was quietly elegant. Her eyes touched lightly over the period fireplace, the four-poster bed, the antique secretary, as if to brand each piece and claim it as her own. French doors opened on to a small balcony jutting into the arms of an elderly cottonwood, and it was from here that she had her first glimpse of the barn. She looked down on a walkway lined with old-fashioned carriage lamps, leading through a hedge that bordered the back lawns to a massive building whose outlines were barely visible in the dark.

'You can visit the barn later if you like,' Robert called, and she turned to go back inside. He stood fidgeting at the foot of her bed, so obviously apprehensive that she felt a sudden impulse to give him a tip. 'I do think we should be getting downstairs, though. Mrs Willers can be a bit harsh when food is left to cool,' he said lamely, and Valerie smothered a giggle at his obvious concern about incurring Willy's wrath.

The house was much larger than it appeared from the outside, and she thought perhaps she should be leaving a trail of crumbs as she followed Robert through half a dozen downstairs rooms to a large, formal dining room. She was about to sit down at the large plank table when Mrs Willers peeked out through a crack in a pair of swinging doors that obviously led to the kitchen.

'I'll need a hand carrying things, Robert,' she said, but Valerie caught a glimpse of the warm room behind her, and responded as if she had been beckoned by an irresistible illusion.

'Mrs Willers, would it be all right if I ate in there?' She inclined her head towards the kitchen.

The older woman praised her with a broad smile as if she had done something very right. 'If you can stand our company, it's certainly all right. Robert and I were going to have a bite in there.'

'I'd appreciate the company. I hate eating alone.'

Valerie couldn't help smiling as she entered the large, farm kitchen with its warm, dark wood and ancient brick hearth. A round oak table by the windows literally groaned under the weight of Mrs Willers' 'light' supper, and the room was fragrant with the smells of recent cooking and freshly perked coffee.

'What a marvellous room,' she said softly, thinking of the contrast to the stainless steel coldness of the brownstone's kitchen.

Robert and Mrs Willers exchanged questioning glances, and she spoke quickly to explain. 'I spent most of my childhood in a very formal dining room dreaming of a kitchen like this.' She felt suddenly foolish, and very unlike the sophisticated, worldly journalist she had intended to appear. At least Rissom wasn't there to see her childlike enchantment with the house, and suddenly she was glad he'd been called away.

She relaxed quickly under Mrs Willers' steady stream of conversation, and even Robert seemed to unbend midway into the meal. She watched him eat uneasily for a time, faintly surprised that such a mechanised man would require food at all, but when she satisfied herself that he at least possessed that one very human characteristic, he seemed much less forbidding.

They lingered over coffee, Mrs Willers detailing the events of the day at the farm, and Valerie finally giving into laughter at Robert's desperate attempts to maintain dignified silence under Willy's merciless teasing.

'He isn't so stiff at home, believe me,' Mrs Willers said at one point, and Valerie's eyebrows raised in a politely unspoken question. 'We live behind the trees there, in our own little cottage,' Willy explained, then seeing the astonishment on Valerie's face, she began to laugh. 'We're married, dear. Robert *Willers*. That's his name.'

Valerie opened her mouth to speak, then clamped it shut abruptly. Whatever she said about the preposterous union of this stiff little man and this wonderfully big, warm woman was bound to be inappropriate. Instead, she thanked them both for the meal, and made an excuse about a walk outside before going to bed.

Mrs Willers patted her arm with a plump hand as she rose. 'There's a phone by your bed, dear. If you need anything, just dial nine. That rings our cottage. I'm not sure how late Charles will get in, but he promised to be here for breakfast.'

She thanked her again and left the house by the back door. Breakfast, indeed, she thought with sudden resentment. And just where was the surprising Mr Rissom spending the night? A business meeting seemed very unlikely out here in the middle of nowhere, and she imagined a shady liaison with a buxom, local farm girl.

She was halfway down the walk towards the barn, rubbing her arms briskly against the deepening night chill, when she saw the figure moving towards her out of the darkness. There was a momentary queasiness as she remembered she was a stranger to the hired hands Willy said lived in apartments over the barn, and then she recognised the long, dark silhouette, the effortless stride, the set of the head on broad, strong shoulders.

She caught her breath quietly in her throat, dismally surprised to feel her body quicken with exactly the same intensity she remembered from months before, just at the sight of him. He moved steadily towards where she had stopped, and came to a halt just far enough from her body to examine the full length of it. His features were barely visible in the light from a distant lamp, but she felt his eyes on her like a lash, flicking from one part of her to another until she was enveloped in the prickling warmth of her own reaction. Then without a word spoken between them, he pulled her savagely into his arms, crushing her mouth under his, drawing the breath from her body with the urgent rush of his hands, and she had to battle the fire building within her to push him away. He had used her in just such a way before, and still been able to leave without so much as a word of parting. She could not allow him to do it again.

She succeeded in making her voice cold, and slightly disdainful. 'Do you greet all your guests with such enthusiasm, Mr Rissom?'

His head jerked back on his shoulders as if he had been slapped, and there was an ominous moment of silence before he relaxed and laughed from deep in his throat. 'It's the way you wanted me to greet you, isn't it?'

She blanched at his arrogant confidence, and at the transparency of her own desire.

'Well, Valerie?' He pulled her back into the circle of one arm and pushed the fingers of his other hand deep into the mass of her hair. 'It's over. You don't have to play games anymore,' he whispered huskily. 'There are no more secrets between us. You can let it all go, give in to what we've both wanted since the first time we saw each other.'

His smile was so peculiar, so boyishly confident of her response, that her indignation increased. 'Take up where we left off, is that what you mean?' She felt his hand move down to circle her throat, and tried desperately not to respond.

'That's exactly what I mean,' he whispered into the hair by her ear. Then he pressed his lips against the side of her throat, and tipping her head to improve his access to the long line of her neck was an involuntary reaction, just like the reflexive arch of her back against his head, and she was powerless to control it.

She would stop him in a minute. She would regain control and reclaim a will of her own, and stop him then. But not just yet. Not while his hands were running over her body with the insistent pressure of possession, not while she could still feel the slow, simmering warmth follow his fingers as they tracked with maddening lightness over her breast and down to her stomach, not until she could breathe again. She had this much coming. She had earned it.

'This is why you invited me here, isn't it?' she breathed, and his hands hesitated at the sound of her voice.

His own voice was thick, and slightly irritated at the distraction from his purpose. 'Of course it is. You didn't think the interview would be free, did you?'

The sentence ended in a playful, impatient tease, as if she were a willing and knowledgeable partner in his twisted version of give and take. She tensed under his hand, hearing the plain-spoken barter, the hallmark of all his damnable business relationships. Fair share for both sides. She would get the interview, he would have use of her body in exchange. It was even worse than she had imagined. She had expected indifference, but he was offering a business deal, and he had calculated the price with a nonchalance that left her cold.

She pushed him away with steady hands. Not the frantic struggle of a woman fighting her own desire, but the cool, measured pressure of resignation, and he recognised the difference.

'Valerie? What's wrong?' His voice was deceptively gentle, and she knew if she listened hard enough, she would come dangerously close to imagining a note of caring. But she had made that mistake before.

'You said there was no need for game-playing,' she said quietly, 'and I'll take you at your word. The Kentucky games are over.' She willed her shoulders to straighten haughtily, and put an icy edge into her voice. 'I didn't come here with any intention of barter. I came here for an interview that was promised. Nothing more. If you want to renege on that promise, please tell me now, and I'll leave in the morning.'

He took a startled step backward, and she felt a tiny pang of satisfaction that at last *she* had surprised *him*.

'That's why you came here?' he asked in disbelief. 'For the interview? Only that?'

'I never expected anything else,' she said evenly. 'I'm amazed that you did.'

He grabbed at her arm and yanked her towards him, his eyes straining to read hers in the dark.

'You're lying,' he said finally, but she could hear the uncertainty in his voice.

'There's no reason to lie anymore,' she said steadily while her legs trembled beneath her. 'You said so yourself.'

His hands grasped either side of her head and his mouth descended with a vicious brutality he had never demonstrated before, as if the intensity of his physical assault could produce the surrender of her mind. She gasped at the force and the sheer animal power of his embrace, but remained passive in his arms, refusing him the satisfaction of knowing he moved her.

Her lack of response was the only reaction he had not been prepared to deal with, and there was an immediate pause in the demanding movements of his lips against hers, then he thrust her roughly from him, as if she were an object whose usefulness had suddenly vanished.

She could hear the angry rasp of breath in his throat as he stood rigid before her, his hands clenched at his sides. At least there was a small victory in having overpowered the demands of her own body, and that victory planted a tiny smile that Charles noticed, and took for disdain.

'Well,' she said, feeling a new confidence strengthen her voice, 'will there be an interview or not?'

He turned his head from her so quickly that his hair flew across his forehead, and in that moment, there was nothing she wanted more than the freedom to reach out and brush it gently to the side. The need to touch him became a physical pain she could barely endure, and for depriving her of that simple pleasure, she hated him.

'What's wrong, Mr Rissom?' she asked bitterly. 'Haven't you ever been turned down before?'

'Let's just say I've never been such a poor judge of character before,' he replied stonily.

His head turned slowly to face her, and even in the dark she could see the dangerous glint of controlled anger in his eyes. The desire was still there. It quivered between them like a taut wire. She was well aware of the awesome power of his control over his own body, knew that he would not demean himself by taking her against her will, and part of her wanted to reach out and shatter that resistance. She wanted him trembling, helpless with his own desire, as desperate for the touch of her hand as she was for his, but she waited too long, and when he spoke, his voice was flat and unemotional, and her chance was gone.

'You'll get your interview,' he said. 'I always keep my promises.'

She heard the back door of the house slam a few seconds later, and it was only then that she fully realised she was alone.

She exhaled a shaky sigh, and tried to convice herself that it was better this way. Better that she knew from the start where she stood in his estimation, even if the realisation had been almost unbearably painful.

It would seem that he considered Valerie Kipper much the same as Valerie Smith—a woman with a price tag. She shook her head angrily against the lone tear that fell on to her cheek. At least he had been willing to pay a high price. The value of her body had apparently been judged equal to the value of his privacy. She would have been the most expensive prostitute in the world.

She avoided a confrontation with Willy and Robert by walking around the house and entering silently by the front door. She ached with an emptiness that sapped her strength and made climbing the stairs to her room an exercise in physical endurance. Indistinct sounds came from the room next to hers, and although she knew Charles was there, she felt no apprehension, no anticipation about spending the night alone with him in his house. He would not cross her threshold tonight. Of that she was certain.

She wakened once during the night to the sound of footsteps pacing the hall outside her door. She lay flat on her back, her eyes wide and sightless in the dark room, holding her breath as the footsteps hesitated by her door. They retreated, then returned, again and again, and she began to share the agony of the struggle taking place on the other side of a door that was only a door, after all, but seemed an impermeable barrier. She awaited the outcome calmly, as if she were only an uninvolved spectator to the quiet battle of will raging just a few feet away, and not a potential participant. When the footsteps retreated for the last time, and she heard the muffled click of the door latch next to hers, all the muscles in her body screamed with the sudden release of prolonged tension, and her eyes closed on the knowledge that she had been waiting. He must have wanted her a great deal to risk a second rejection. At least she had that much.

Charles was already seated at the dining-room table when she came down the next morning. In the space of a second his glance took in the clothes she had chosen carelessly, so painfully aware of her own body that the covering she placed on it seemed pathetically unimportant. She wore snug, fading jeans, so long familiar with her legs that they reflected her shape even on the hanger, and a soft, bulky sweater the same periwinkle blue as Jacob's eyes. She had clutched the sweater to her breast like a child's security blanket before pulling it over her head. Thinking of Jacob fortified her somehow, and after last night, the marriage proposal he renewed with every phone call seemed more attractive than ever.

Charles was dressed similarly, except his sweater was off-white, accentuating his dark complexion, making him look foreign, and almost sinister. There was a catch in her throat as he rose from the table to greet her. She had never pictured Charles Rissom in jeans that spoke of countless washings and long wear, and suddenly the captain of industry faded away, and she faced a simple, country man whose eyes reached out to twist her heart.

'Good morning,' he said with a courteous smile, and she closed her eyes against everything the smile conveyed. She had seen it a hundred times before, the gracious greeting of host to guest, like the façade of storefronts in an old Western town, propped up by sticks and one-sided, with nothing behind it.

'Good morning,' she answered sadly, and returned a smile as empty as his.

'Willy already left for the market,' he announced with apparent good humour, 'but she outdid herself with the breakfast spread. All in your honour, incidentally. It would seem she took quite a shine to you last night.'

Valerie slid into the chair opposite his and sagged against the ladder back. This, then, would be the ultimate punishment. That he could forget the raging desire of the night before, shrug it away as if it had never existed, and slip easily into his new role as gracious host.

He moved casually to the sideboard flanking one wall and began lifting covers from an appallingly long row of chafing dishes. 'I'm afraid you'll have to sample a bit of everything, or Willy will take offence, so I won't even offer you a choice, do you mind?' He smiled as he held a serving spoon poised over one dish, and Valerie shook her head mutely. 'In this house,' he continued conversationally, 'we try to avoid offending Willy at all costs. She's the one who keeps it all together.'

Valerie frowned as she watched him fill her plate. She had been fully prepared for his hostility after her rejection of his advances, but not for his indifference. It was impossible for her to pretend she was unaffected, and she bitterly resented his nonchalance. He had nearly destroyed her, and yet he remained unscathed. She wanted desperately to hurt him.

'Where were you last night?' she demanded suddenly, and as soon as the words were out of her mouth, she realised that they sounded possessive. She waited for him to tell her it was none of her business, and for a moment he paused in the motions of filling her plate as if he would. But instead he merely smiled and returned to the table, placing a plate heaped with an assortment of food before her.

'Not out chasing local farm girls, if that's what you thought,' he answered easily.

She blushed furiously, because he had intuitively known what she was thinking, and because his amusement was obvious.

'A neighbour of mine almost lost a fine broodmare to colic yesterday. We spent all afternoon and a good part of the evening walking her through it. It was an emergency, or I would have met your plane myself. I apologise if it seemed rude.'

The gracious host again. His excellence at the role was beginning to irritate her.

'Is there something else you'd prefer? You're not eating.'

Her eyes flashed at him across the table. 'I would prefer it if you were a little less solicitous!' she snapped. She stabbed viciously at her plate with her fork, feeling no appetite at all.

'I'm sorry,' he said effortlessly, and she knew he was not sorry at all. 'What would you like me to be, if not solicitous?' His eyes flickered with interest.

The question hung between them like a tether ball that could swing in either direction, and she closed her eyes briefly in exasperation. 'Yourself,' she said finally. 'I'd like you to be yourself.'

'And would you recognise it if I were?' he asked quietly, and she met his eyes openly with the only admission she could afford.

'I don't know. Probably not,' she mumbled. 'So far this visit has revealed only one thing: that I don't know you at all.'

He locked his hands behind his head and leaned back in his chair, infuriatingly at ease. 'Well, that's what you're here for, isn't it? To get to know me, and tell the world what I am?'

He rocked forward and leaned on his arms, his eyes on hers curiously. 'What would you tell your readers now, if you were to write the article this morning? How would you describe Charles Rissom?'

'As a manager,' she answered instantly. 'Of people, horses, industry, everything. That's what Charles Rissom is. A manager.'

He raised his eyebrows. 'That's a pretty one-dimensional portrait. You were kinder to Charles Smith.'

'Charles Smith was a fictitious person,' she retorted. 'I made him up.'

'Just like you made up Valerie Smith?' His stare was so intense that she dropped her eyes.

'Valerie.' The word was a command, and she looked up slowly, helpless to disobey. 'What you see here is Charles Rissom,' he said softly. 'And Charles Smith. This place, the people around me, the life I live here— it's all there is of me, and all I ever want to be. You were the only person I ever wanted to see it.'

Her words dripped like acid on a steel plate. 'Just like I was the only person to ever hear the Martin Vasslar story?'

He laughed out loud, but the sound was harsh, and unpleasant. 'The liar dares to condemn a lie!' he said bitterly. 'Don't forget, Ms Kipper, you were the one who started the chain of deception. I merely followed your lead. When I found out I had told one of the country's top journalists who I was, it became necessary to plant a little false information, just in case you did publish a story that exposed me as Charles Smith. The Vasslar nonsense would have ruined your credibility, and then the rest of your story would have been unbelievable, too. I was simply protecting myself.'

'You knew who I was?' she whispered, and her face reflected dismayed astonishment. 'All that time?'

He met her eyes steadily. 'Robert recognised you at the restaurant. I had your dossier by the next morning.'

'And so you planned to plant a false story that would ruin my career,' she accused him.

'Just as you used a false identity to ruin my privacy,' he said calmly.

Her shoulders sagged and she let her head fall back on her neck, relinquishing her tenuous hold on self-righteousness. 'All right,' she admitted finally, 'we both lied. The score is tied.'

'Yes, it is,' he said quietly.

'You knew then, all along, that Jacob and I were not lovers?' She had to force the words out of her throat, and still they sounded small and weak.

He sighed and looked down at the table. 'I was never really sure about that. Just because you were Valerie Kipper didn't mean you couldn't be involved with Jacob. But he told me himself, after Kentucky.' His eyes grew hard as she watched them. 'He also told me that he still wanted to marry you, in spite of your attempts to convince him otherwise.'

She nodded silently.

'Well? Do you intend to marry him?'

She looked up quickly, imagining she heard the same possessive tone she had heard in her own voice earlier, when she asked him where he had been the night before, but his face was closed, and reflected only mild interest.

'I don't know,' she answered honestly. 'I'm considering it.'

He nodded and turned his face away for a moment, and every part of her ached to reach out and touch him.

'Will you tell me something?' she asked softly.

'Of course. What is it?'

'Why did you wait so long to invite me here?'

'I was waiting for your story on the Egyptian Event,' he said flatly. 'To see if you'd betray my confidence. When you didn't, it said something about you. I probably read more into it than was there, but that was my mistake, not yours.'

'So the interview is my reward for not exposing you as Charles Smith.' The statement was flat and dull, as if the words had no substance.

'You could put it that way, I suppose. Although it was intended to be more than that.'

The oblique reference to his proposition of the night before saddened her, and she smiled ruefully at the memory of all the fairytales, at her childish notion of happy endings, and she put away forever the worn conviction that she would know love when she saw it. It didn't make the pain less as she raised her eyes to look at him, but it dissolved the anger, and without that, she was empty.

'At least we both know where we stand now,' she said with a shrug, and he responded with a thin smile.

'So the interview begins now, is that it?'

'Yes. The interview begins now.'

'Fine.' He slapped a hand on the table in punctuation, and she jumped. 'If you'd like to wait for me in the barn, the grooms will show you around. We'll start there. I have a few calls to make, but I'll join you shortly.'

She looked down at her plate as he left the room, feeling suddenly guilty that she had eaten so little. Willy would be disappointed. It was strangely important at that moment that someone in that house be fond of her, and she took a last token bite in a twisted, symbolic attempt to insure Willy's affection. It was a childish, ridiculous gesture, and she knew it. The food was dry and tasteless because she hadn't wanted it, and she was halfway across the back lawn on her way to the barn before she swallowed.

When she passed through the narrow opening in the hedge that bordered the yard, she stopped in amazement, startled by her sudden emergence into a landscape that reminded her for the first time that she was in the presence of great wealth. There was no subtlety in the enormous, oval pool that lay at the bottom of a slope to her right, yet on the other side of the hedge, she would never have guessed at its existence. Flaring metallic beams arched high over the water, and she recognised the low, bulky housing on one side as a storage place for the transparent dome that would enclose the pool in winter. The thought of swimming outside in the middle of a Minnesota snowstorm was preposterously extravagant, and her jaw dropped at the eccentricity. There were tennis courts beyond the pool, and at this comparatively moderate expense, she merely nodded. Charles Rissom may play at modest country living, she thought, but he certainly does it with style.

She followed the left fork in the walkway to the looming structure of an old-fashioned barn that duplicated the turn-of-the-century architecture of the house. It was fully one hundred feet long and over half as wide, and the interior smelled pleasantly of sweet hay and sawdust. Yet even here, as in the house, the façade of simple country living masked a luxury afforded by very few. She passed a large control panel with switches regulating temperature throughout the various sections of the barn's massive interior, and eight blank televisions monitors provided constant supervision of all of the foaling stalls.

A lanky young man of uncertain age introduced himself shyly as Eddie, and led the way through the barn's massive midsection to a wing on one side.

'The indoor arena's on the other side,' he explained amicably, pausing to push at the mop of bright red hair that fell continually over his eyes. 'But the horses are all stabled in here.' He pushed open a wide plank door and allowed her to pass through before him. 'Normally they'd all be out to pasture by this time, but Mr Rissom wanted you to see them first.' There was a mild admonishment in his voice, as if he were holding her personally responsible for keeping the horses locked in past their scheduled time.

There were six mares with jittery, energetic foals dancing in roomy box stalls, exhibiting their youthful impatience to be out at play. Each one was more enchanting than the last, pushing tiny muzzles fearlessly against her hand as she reached over the stall doors.

'They're turning into pets, instead of show horses,' he said, and there was a note of impatience in his voice. She examined his troubled frown, and guessed that Jacob's influence had already marked the boy. Here was another eager showman, waiting for his chance in centre ring, thinking of horses only as the means to further the exhibition of the man, instead of the other way around. She had buttonholed Jacob without realising it, and the sudden revelation of what inspired the man made her raise her eyebrows in surprise.

Eventually the tour ended at a closed door that blocked off another section of the barn. 'The stallion's in there,' Eddie explained, and turned to walk back the way they had come.

'What stallion?' she asked quickly, remaining at the door, refusing to move.

Eddie turned with an expression of exasperation. '*The* stallion. Sheikh el Din.'

She shook her head and frowned. 'I thought he was

supposed to stand at the other farm, Juniper Farm, with Jacob.'

'That's what we all thought, but Mr Rissom yanked him off the show circuit in June, and brought him home. He didn't service many outside mares stuck up here, that's for sure. And he lost a shot at the national championship.' Eddie's voice was clearly disapproving.

'Why?' she asked quietly, and the boy rolled his eyes.

'Who knows why? The only thing Mr Rissom would say was something about keeping the things that mattered with him all the time.'

She closed her eyes tightly and sighed. 'Can I go in there?'

Eddie pursed his lips uncertainly. 'Well, he *is* a stallion, you know. And he's loose in there. It's just a big, open stall where he can run in and out from the pasture. Mr Rissom won't keep him locked up.'

'It's all right,' she smiled. 'Sheikh and I are old friends.' And with that she opened the door and walked through, closing it quickly behind her. Eddie's eyes widened in surprise, and he stood frozen for only a moment before leaping to the door and rushing after her.

'Listen, ma'am,' he said breathlessly as he secured the latch, 'you can't come in here alone. Like I said, the horse is *loose*.' His emphasis on the last word clearly implied that the animal was dangerous, and that she was a fool, but Valerie wasn't paying attention.

She crossed the wide stall and stood framed in the opening to the rolling pasture, searching the green and gold hills impatiently with her eyes.

Charles came quietly through the door, took in the scene, and glanced sternly at Eddie. The boy merely shrugged helplessly, his body language indicating that his employer's guest was totally beyond his control, and deserved whatever consequences would follow.

As if to emphasise his silent judgment, there was a

distant thunder of pounding hooves, and a dark head with mane flying appeared over the ridge of the first hill. The three-beat gait sounded like a distant drum, becoming louder and louder as the galloping apparition bore down on the tiny figure immobilised in the doorway.

Just as Charles had taken the first lunging stride of a run that would put his body between Valerie and the horse, Sheikh slid to a quivering halt, his ears pricked forward, his nostrils blowing low, suspicious whistles at the stranger in his territory. His head poised high on the coil of his neck, the muscles of his flank rippled in readiness to either attack or flee, he took a few tentative steps forward. Then his tail flew skyward in the high flag of recognition, and he trotted towards Valerie, piercing the morning air with a whinny of greeting.

'Well, I'll be damned,' Eddie said softly as he watched Sheikh bury his head in Valerie's arms, but when he looked to his employer for an explanation, Charles was already across the stall, at Valerie's side, watching in silent amazement as the tears coursed freely down her face.

CHAPTER FOURTEEN

WILLY stood with one hip jutting out, her fist planted firmly in the cushion of flesh at her waist, her face a study in exasperation. 'You haven't eaten a decent meal in two days,' she complained, morosely watching Charles pick at the food on his plate. 'And neither has Valerie. Where is she, anyway?'

'She's packing, Willy, and you're mothering again.'

She narrowed her eyes at the little line that appeared between Charles' brows. It always warned her when she had gone too far, when the words she had left to say were better left unsaid, but this time she didn't care.

'Well somebody had better mother you two, or you'll starve yourselves to death!' She beat viciously at the eggs in the pan and muttered just loud enough for Charles to hear, 'I don't know why being in love should ruin an appetite anyway. It's nonsense, pure and simple.'

Charles looked up sharply and narrowed his eyes at her back. 'Who's in love?' he demanded.

She whirled on him with the spoon still in her hand, dripping egg batter onto the immaculate floor. 'Don't play word games with me, Charles Rissom! There've been enough word games between the two of you this weekend to last me a lifetime!'

Charles smiled bitterly at the truth of her remark, and scolded her gently. 'You're an enormous cross to bear, Willy, you know that? All over the world people treat me with deference, respect, even fear. But in my own home, I'm bullied mercilessly by a madwoman who drips egg on the floor.'

Her eyes jumped to the spoon in her hand, and then to the scattered drops on the floor, and she grumbled an

178

uncharacteristic curse as she bent to wipe up the spill. 'This is your fault, you know,' she said from the floor, and Charles smiled at her fondly, which for some reason increased her irritation. 'If I weren't so upset by the two of you, I'd be able to keep my mind on my business.' She stood quickly, her round face flushed, and looked him squarely in the eye. 'You shouldn't let her leave,' she said firmly. 'You want her here, and if you weren't four kinds of a fool, you'd tell her that.'

He returned her stare quietly, deciding that Willy was much too perceptive for his tastes at the moment. 'If you must know, I tried to tell her that the very first night, Willy,' he said crossly. 'She made it quite clear then that the idea didn't appeal to her at all, that she came here for the interview and nothing else.'

His voice was unusually harsh, and she bristled at the tone. 'Then she was lying. Any fool could see that just by looking at the way she looks at you.'

'Then maybe the fool is looking too hard, and seeing only what she wants to see. And please bear in mind that there's a very fine line between mothering and meddling. You're coming dangerously close to crossing it!'

His face closed to her as he left by the back door, and she stood staring after him in open-mouthed astonishment.

Upstairs, Valerie folded the last blouse carefully, and snapped the suitcase shut on neat stacks of clothing she had never worn. She'd spent most of the last two days in jeans and sweatshirts, and had found no use for the more formal items she had packed back in New York, when she was determined to be prepared for anything.

But you weren't prepared for this, she thought sadly. Not for the house, not for Willy, or even for Robert, funny in his formality like Uncle John was funny in his gruffness, trying to reach out through the barriers of propriety to demonstrate affection. Poor Robert had actually patted her on the shoulder last night after supper, and then looked at his own hand, horrified that it has breached his rigid code of conduct. Leaving just that much behind was hard enough, leaving Charles Rissom with it, for the very last time, was very nearly unbearable.

She flung herself down on the bed and stared up at the ceiling, torturing herself with the memory of the last two days. Just this one time, she promised herself. I'll think of it all just one last time, then I'll put it away, leave this place, and pull myself together.

Charles had not asked her about her tearful reunion with Sheikh, even though she knew he hadn't understood it, and she loved him for that. She had barely understood it herself, this peculiar relationship with an animal that would have terrified her only months before. But she and Sheikh were alike: both vibrant, loving spirits, trapped by the games men played, longing to be free. And they both loved Charles, and only Charles had the power to free them. Perhaps that was why meeting Sheikh again had cracked the dam that released the emotional torrent. He was free at last, and she wasn't.

She had cried and cried, and although Charles said nothing, and asked no questions, eventually his arms had wrapped around her in a comforting embrace, and their relationship changed. His empathy for her feelings about his horse had at least earned her his friendship, and for two days she basked in the warmth of a fond affection she had never felt from him before. There was a childlike innocence in the way they related, sharing the time as if there were no tomorrow, but without the desperate, time-passing urgency of adults.

They had played in the pool, had ferociously competitive tennis matches, and both of them teased Robert unmercifully, laughing about it later like naughty children. And through it all they talked endlessly, about philosophy, politics, religion, and eventually, themselves. He knew as much about her life as she knew about his, and was remarkably perceptive about her moods and feelings, with one glaring exception. He didn't know she loved him. She had done that very well.

She paused in her reverie, listening to the distant sounds of activity from outside her bedroom window. She heard the sharp crack of Charles' voice carry across the morning air, and just the sound of it made her curl inward, and rock against the pain of never hearing the voice again.

They had made one last tour of the barn last night, and although she had promised herself that she wouldn't, she cried again when Sheikh nuzzled her hand for the last time. Her shoulders shook with the force of the sobs she was helpless to control, and Charles stood by awkwardly, somehow sensing that there was no comfort for this sorrow, and that he had no place in it. In her farewell to the stallion, she cried her farewell to Charles, and he never knew it.

But when she finally turned to him, her cheeks streaked with tears, her heart on her face for anyone who cared to look, he said the most remarkable thing. 'He's yours, if you want him,' he said softly, and she knew the measure of that gift, and that he meant it. She looked down at the floor and shook her head silently, and nothing he said could make her speak again while they were still in the barn.

It was much later when they sat in the comfortable silence of friendship on the front porch, as Charles pushed the swing with regular taps of his foot on the floor, postponing the moment when they would finally go to their separate rooms, and end the last day.

She was curled up on one leg to face him, her hand resting casually behind his head, and it seemed the most natural thing in the world for her fingers to stray to the vibrant cluster of black hair and twist a lock gently around her thumb. Her eyes were on that lock of hair, and she didn't see his own fly open at the touch of her hand.

He stiffened slightly, and spoke in measured, mechanical tones. 'Do you have all you need for the story?' he asked quietly.

'More than enough. More than you probably wanted to give me,' she answered absently, still fascinated with the lifelike qualities of the curl that seemed to cling to her fingers with a will of its own. She had never touched him. In two days, she had never touched him intentionally, and now that she started, she couldn't seem to stop. The faint ping of a warning bell in the back of her mind was lost in her earnest concentration on her hand, and she watched it move like a separate entity, her head cocked, her mouth open in the drugged stupor of fascination. Her hand dropped to his shoulder, and drew a tiny circle around a design on his shirt, and she had no conscious knowledge of doing it. He never moved, never stopped the steady push of his foot that kept the swing in motion, never once indicated that he was even aware of her touch.

'When will it be published?' he asked, and his voice cracked slightly.

'Never,' she answered lazily, lulled by the swing and the feel of his body beneath her hand, forgetting that she hadn't intended to tell him that. And then she realised what she had said aloud, and pulled her hand away just as he stopped the swing abruptly with his foot.

'Why not?' he asked roughly, and he grabbed her hand and squeezed unconsciously, as if the pressure would force the answer from her palm, and as if the answer were the most important thing in the world.

She frowned at the narrowed intensity of his eyes as he peered into hers, and answered quickly, pulling her hand away from the painful pressure.

'I don't know,' she said defensively, rising from the swing to lean out over the porch railing. 'Maybe because

I'm selfish. Maybe because I don't want the world to have this.' She swept out an arm that encompassed the farm, the house, and all it contained, and turned to face him. 'The world doesn't deserve it,' she finished softly, and if her eyes had ever spoken, they were speaking now, and she didn't care if he saw the pain.

His push off the swing brought his body up to face hers, and with the tortured slowness of a man fighting his own intentions, his hands lifted to her face and cradled it between them. His eyes never met hers, but followed the movements of his hands as they moved through her hair, threading deep into the thickness of it until his fingers pressed against her skull. She watched his face reflect waves of emotion that passed over his features, changing them constantly, until his eyes shifted downwards and locked on hers. And then she was drowning in the liquid pool of his gaze, and the battle was lost, and her body surrendered peacefully to a fate that could no longer be denied. His lips touched hers lightly, again and again in kisses that cherished, pulling her eyes closed like a blind on reason. She heard herself whimper against the forces that commanded her, and as if the sound had by itself shattered whatever remnants of control remained, his mouth became hard and demanding, moving against hers with an urgency that broke her breathing into quick, shallow gasps. She raised her arms to wrap around his neck, and they seemed to move in slow motion, accentuating the movement of her breasts under her sweater as they rose to meet him. When her hands found each other at the back of his neck, he grabbed convulsively at her waist and pulled her towards him. When he felt her breasts flatten against him, and felt the length of her thigh meet his and press into it, he threw his head back and drew in a great gulp of air, like a man who is drowning.

With the last vestige of will he ever hoped to have, or could have been expected to have, he pushed her away from his body and held her there with hands that trembled on her shoulders. Her lips were parted with the force of air she drew deeply into her lungs, and her eyes were wide, and deep, and pleading. His own breathing was ragged and forced, and his voice was unrecognisable. 'Do you want this?' he demanded hoarsely, and her body quivered 'under his hands like a bowstring pulled taut.

'Yes,' she breathed, never taking her eyes from his.

'Just this one night?' he persisted, and she twisted away from his hands and pushed herself against him, willing to accept this on any terms he would name, no longer caring that one night was all he would offer, all she would ever have.

'Just this one night,' she agreed huskily, and as her hands slipped under his sweater to twist through the hairs on his chest, he groaned in an anguish that rose from his throat and tightened his face with the harsh lines of sorrow.

But she never saw his face. Not until later, after he had lifted her effortlessly and carried her down the porch steps, and placed her gently on the soft cushion of lawn. And then she watched him breathlessly as he knelt on the grass beside her, endlessly fascinated by the lights in his eyes that burned like lasers over each part of her body he uncovered. When she finally lay naked before him, a glowing, willing offering on the altar of his desire, he rocked back on his heels and coveted the whole of her body with his eyes, his fingers suspended over the throbbing fullness of her left breast as if he were afraid to touch it.

As he bent to press his lips against the softness of her shoulder, his hair fell over his face and brushed across the peak of a mound reaching for him, calling up a rush of fiery heat that tore through her body and escaped her throat in a tiny cry. Then his hand slid down to press flat against her stomach, and she coiled against him, pulsing with her need, demanding the union she had waited all her life to find, putting away the aching reminder that this was all she would have. At that moment, with his face etched above her against the blackness of the sky, it seemed enough.

There had been no shame afterward, and no words between them as he carried her up the stairs, her head bobbing against his shoulder like that of a sleepy child. And she had felt the trusting contentment of a child as he lay her gently on the bed, tucking the covers around her, bending at last to press his lips tenderly against her closing eyes. He straightened slowly and smiled down on the serenity of her face, tightening his eyes in an empty sadness that lingered only briefly, and watched her fall asleep.

There was a sharp clatter from downstairs as Willy dropped something in the kitchen, and Valerie sat up on the bed quickly. She felt suddenly empty, as if remembering the last two days had used up the memory, and there was nothing left. She looked around the room one last time before closing the door softly behind her, then she carried her suitcases down the stairs herself.

'Willy,' she said later as she stood by the front door, her hand on the knob, the muted rumble of a car engine calling her outside. 'I know this sounds silly after only two days, and I don't care. I love you. In fact I think I loved you from the very first time I saw you.' She pushed the words out with her lips angrily, forcing them out of hiding.

But then it felt so good to give love out loud, that suddenly she wanted to give it to everyone, to relieve the pressure of too much of it held inside. 'And you can tell Robert that I love him too, whether he likes it or not,' she finished defiantly, her eyes brimming. And tell the house, and tell the horses, and tell the woods and the river, but whatever you do, don't tell Charles, she finished the thought in her mind.

Willy's merry, round face crumpled immediately, and she swept Valerie into the pillow of her arms, and said with them what she couldn't say, for once, with words. Then she rushed away quickly, one chubby hand digging into an apron pocket for the lace handkerchief she knew she had tucked there this morning, and Valerie was left to pass through the door alone.

Charles stood next to the car, waiting for her to emerge from the house. His expression was dark and forbidding, much as it had been as he stood over her last night, drinking in the sight of her while she slept, allowing his emotions free play over his face only because she couldn't see them. He swallowed the catch in his throat as he saw her hesitate on the porch, framed in its outline, thinking how right it was that she should be standing there, and how much she belonged to this place. And then the anguish of the night before washed over him in an ugly wave, and his heart tightened against her.

He had stood over her bed for nearly an hour, watching her breasts rise and fall in the sweet, untroubled sleep of the innocent, baffled by her ability to let go so easily, to slip blissfully away from all that had passed between them. When he finally returned to his own room, he had paced away most of the night, building an anger that what he had felt could be absorbed, and used, then casually thrust away.

The depth of his feeling was so great, that he refused to believe she would not return it. So he had asked her in desperation, 'Just this one night?', and had willed her to say forever, but for the first time in his life, his will had not been enough. 'Just this one night,' she had answered, and though his mind cried out against it, his body was past caring, and he took all she would give him.

His smile was thin and bitter as she walked up to the

car, and stared at him over the roof before opening the door. 'I'm ready to leave now,' she said softly, and he answered her with sarcasm.

'I'll just bet you are.'

The shame was upon her then, colouring her face as she climbed into the car. She had heard the contempt in his voice, and knew that last night had erased any tenuous friendship they had shared. She had proved him right, demonstrated beyond all doubt that she was really no different than any other woman he had known, because she had surrendered to his terms. His was a peculiar, self-righteous morality, she thought, one that seduced women and then held them in contempt when they finally weakened, and resentment climbed over her sorrow on the long, silent ride to the airport.

'Well, I hope you're satisfied,' she said bitterly as they pulled into the parking lot, releasing some of the anger that had been rolling to a boil during the wretched, endless silence of the drive. 'You finally got what you wanted.'

'And so did you,' he returned caustically, picking up the conversation as if it had been continuing for hours.

She exhaled sharply through her nostrils, indignation sweeping across the final pangs of regret as they came to a stop near the terminal.

There it was: the gateway to a world without him, and the ache of leaving fought against the rage at him for wanting her to go, and her brow wrinkled in a furious attempt to stop the tears.

'You're a user, you know that?' she almost shouted, and he turned his head slowly to look at her with disdain.

'Then we were very well matched, weren't we?'

She slammed her door so hard that the car rocked under the impact, and watched with her lips pushed out as he pulled her bags from the boot. The lid crashed down with a terrible force, and he turned rudely away from her and began walking towards the terminal, forcing her to run with short, mincing steps to catch up with him.

He checked her baggage with cool dispatch, smiling courteously at the girl who waited on him, going through all the motions, business as usual, as though she were not behind him, burning with rage, her throat tight against the scream that clamoured to get out.

'I'll see you to your departure gate,' he said coldly as he turned from the counter, and something inside gave way with a slow, ripping sound she heard in her ears.

'The hell you will!' she shouted, and dozens of heads turned in her direction, seeking out the blast of sound that sliced the muted rumble of the crowded terminal, the same sound that had slapped Charles Rissom's head back on his shoulders like a physical blow.

She quivered with anger, her chin dropped near her chest as she looked up from eyes hooded with menace. 'So you'll see me to my gate, will you?' she said acidly. 'And watch me board and see me safely out of your life, is that it? You can't wait to see me gone, can you?' Her words came out with the sharp hiss of a deadly snake, rising gradually until the force of them blew across his astonished face like a hot desert wind. 'You hate me because I wanted you!' she shouted, and now a crowd began to gather around them. 'well, you wanted me just as much, so you'd better hate yourself, too! You're only anxious for me to leave because I remind you of your own weakness! I remind you that the almighty Charles Rissom is just as human as the rest of us!'

Ears pricked up and eyebrows raised at the mention of his name, but Valerie didn't notice her audience. She stood planted firmly before him, her chin pointed up towards his face in stiff defiance, her narrowed eyes gleaming with the satisfaction his open-mouthed amazement gave her.

'You don't like hearing it out loud, do you? You don't like your women throwing it all in your face, refusing to walk meekly away when you're finished with them!'

Her voice sounded shrill in her own ears, and she paused to look at him, and to rest a throat that hurt from her harsh use of it. She thought she saw a softening in his features, a gentle tug that pulled down at his eyes and touched the corners of his lips. She thought she saw it, whether it was there nor not, and the thought was enough.

Suddenly the anger was gone, and the colour seeped from her face with it, until all that remained was a thin, pale sheet of determination that made her look stiff, and slightly unreal, like a mannequin. The words were out of her mouth before she could stop them.

'Dammit, Charles Rissom. I love you. Don't you know that?' She shook her head at the futility of what she was saying. 'I've always loved you, since that very first night.'

'What?' His voice was an incredulous whisper.

She nodded sharply and now her voice was filled with self-derision. 'Why did you think I didn't print the story? Why do you think I came to your blasted farm? Why do you think last night happened?'

He started to speak but her eyes flashed a warning and she held up her hand. 'Don't say a thing,' she cautioned him bitterly. 'I've said it all to myself a thousand times, for all the good it did me. No one falls in love in one night, but I did, and there it is.'

He shook his head slowly, and his eyebrows lifted as a smile pulled at his mouth. 'The very first night . . .' he mused. 'You should have told me.'

'Told you what?' she demanded. 'Guess what, Mr Rissom, I'm a reporter trying to trick you into an exclusive, but since I love you, I won't use it? Is that what I should have said?'

He tipped his head back and laughed aloud, and she slumped before him like a rag doll. She noted his laughter with a sadness that welled up from deep inside, and never seemed to stop. '*That's* why I didn't tell you,' she said quietly, and turned to walk away.

The crowd that had gathered parted silently for her exit, and she passed through them blindly, tears streaming down her cheeks. An extraordinary silence hung over the busy terminal, and faces touched with compassion turned darkly on Charles, and marked him with the condemnation of their stares.

But he never saw them. He saw only Valerie, and watched with a bewildered expression as she walked away, numbed by the feeling of pain falling away like an old coat he had worn too long. He felt foolish, and giddy, and warm, and a hundred other things he had never felt before. His face cracked into a broad grin, and he nodded at the people standing around him, feeling suddenly that they were all very old friends that he hadn't seen in a long time, and that it was right that they should be a part of this. For the first time in his life, he was consumed by a feeling too big to hold inside, and all thoughts of privacy fled as his face cleared and his voice boomed across the terminal to touch the tiny figure rushing away. 'Valerie Kipper! I love you too!' And then, as an afterthought, 'Since the very first night!'

The words penetrated slowly, and she stopped, hesitating, then turned to face him. She was still close enough for him to see the look of wonder pass from her eyes to her mouth, and a tiny smile lifted and pulled at his heart. Then the smile vanished and the eyes grew stern in one last, angry reprimand. 'Why didn't you say so?' she shouted back.

There was a long pause, an endless pause, as Valerie waited with a captive audience of strangers to hear his reply. All eyes were on Charles, and the air in the hushed terminal crackled in anticipation.

He stood there for what seemed like a very long time, rigidly intent on only one figure in that frozen sea of figures, and then he shrugged sheepishly and shouted back, 'Because it was private!'

And then the murmuring started, and the soft laughter started, and Valerie was in his arms, exactly where she belonged, and strangers smiled on them fondly, somehow sensing that what they had witnessed was the happy ending to a very private fairytale.